Yeshua, the Untold Story

Yeshua, the Untold Story

LEE CARTER THOMAS

RESOURCE *Publications* · Eugene, Oregon

YESHUA, THE UNTOLD STORY

Resource Publications
An Imprint of Wipf and Stock Publishers
199 W. 8th Ave., Suite 3
Eugene, OR 97401

www.wipfandstock.com

PAPERBACK ISBN: 978-1-7252-9774-6
HARDCOVER ISBN: 978-1-7252-9763-0
EBOOK ISBN: 978-1-7252-9773-9

03/15/21

For Mom, 1940–2019

Contents

Acknowledgments

LET ME BEGIN WITH a series of acknowledgments. First and foremost, I want to acknowledge you, the reader, for giving this book your time and attention. It is not something I take for granted in a world where time is a precious commodity, and several things are competing for our attention. Thank you for choosing to give your attention to this book even if you do not decide to read its contents or purchase it. However, if you read this book, it is an act of faith and a gesture of grace. For that reason, I am even more grateful to you.

But I also need to make another critical acknowledgment. This book is not for everyone—perhaps the most important thing to recognize. Biblical fiction is a growing area of literature for those who wish to expand their imagination about narratives in the Bible and free them from orthodoxy entanglements. It is for those who see the truth revealed in sacred Scripture as organic and evolving. For example, the parable of the talents as told by Jesus in Matthew challenges us to resist becoming the servant who assumed wrongly the master's instructions by saying, *I knew you to be a hard man, reaping where you did not sow and gathering where you scattered no seed*, and out of fear buried his one talent. Like talents, texts have always been subject to revisions, redactions, and recasting for new situations. Jesus often said, "it has been said in old, but now I say unto you. . ." Biblical literalists are sometimes like servants who misinterpret the nature of Scripture as truth to be buried in history and never to be changed. If this is you, this book may not be for you.

Given the first two acknowledgments, the third may come as a surprise. I grew up in a Christian home in North Carolina. My father was a Baptist deacon, my deceased mother the church's pianist and lead soloist. I was ordained a Baptist minister in 1994 and had an extensive career in teaching other Christian ministers. After teaching full-time for eighteen years at a seminary in Oklahoma that did not provide sabbatical time to write and publish, my wife and I decided to move to South Carolina to re-boot our careers and explore our creative writing possibilities. By then, I had grown reluctant and weary in associating myself with the dominant group in the United States who call themselves Christians.

Many who identify themselves in this way are often absorbed by the cultures of commercialism, politics, and individualism. I resolved to call myself simply a follower of Jesus. Labels are not important to me. Now, truth, justice, and equality for all of God's creatures, as seen through the love of Jesus in the Bible and experienced in daily living, have become more essential than being identified with a group, religious or otherwise. Since childhood, I have had a love for the Scriptures and their wisdom about what it means to be human, humble, and divine. Because of this, I did not take writing this book likely.

My sincere hope is that reading this fictional account about a man called Jesus will stir your curiosity about the Bible, not add to the present illiteracy or apathy about Scripture. For instance, the portrayal in the book of Jesus' encounter with the woman at the well will provoke more interest in the New Testament with a new sense of curiosity, reflection, and faithfulness. My intentions are not to rewrite the gospel or introduce a pseudo-hermeneutic. It is to invoke imagination and renewed interest in who Jesus is in the unfolding, flawed, and incomplete human experience. I warn you: a fully embodied, human Jesus will be experienced in this reading.

Although crucial, these series of acknowledgments pale in comparison to the gratitude I have for the important people who helped make this work complete. To my life partner and spouse, Alexis, thank you for believing in me enough to support this work, share the risks, and the celebrations of its success or failure. Your unconditional love and acceptance will always overwhelm my soul. There are too many other friends and colleagues who supported this work than there are pages to write. Thank you for your supportive listening to my audacious ideas and wild imagination.

Prologue

"WHAT IF?" THE TWO most transformative words in the English language. A simple question that often leads to invention, innovation, and constructive change. All major social movements start with the question "What if?" Institutions are built and dismantled at the mere mention of those words. But few places allow the utterance of the question "What if?" Most prefer, even demand, the statement "What is" instead, as was the case at the St. Paul Baptist Church, where Ramon Richardson attended weekly Sunday School and bible study.

St. Paul Baptist Church, located in Lynchburg, Virginia's moderately sized town, was like many—sprawling suburbs, divided along racial and economic lines, and deeply steeped in Southern religious heritage. This church was home to many of its city's elites. It was not only the place for Christian folk to gather and forget about the outside world's imperfections, but a museum to preserve the culture and memorialize its heroes. To do this, every Sunday morning at 9:30 a.m., the Sunday school class met in the same room at the end of the hallway in the education building. It was a class where adults could discuss the faith's central tenets and debate their scriptural integrity.

Ramon had always been a deep thinker, to the point of obsession. As a high school science teacher and Christian, he enjoyed attending Sunday school. The lesson that morning was about the apostle Paul's teaching about Jesus and the resurrection. The resurrection had always fascinated Ramon's scientific curiosity. The Bible was not specific about how the resurrection of Jesus occurred. There were no eye-witness accounts. The book of Mark didn't include a resurrection story.

Being familiar with all the theological arguments for and against the resurrection, Ramon understood the difference between resurrection and resuscitation. Still, he wondered about the implications for what happens to us when we die. What if Jesus was never physically resurrected? Is resurrection only an existential reality? His scientific mind doubted its validity.

After recently turning fifty years old, it had become more difficult for him to reconcile his many conflicting preoccupations. Religion and science were not Ramon's only interests. He also loved pop culture, especially when it came to pop music. Even his teenage obsessions with musical icons such as Prince, Michael Jackson, and Cher impacted his theological beliefs.

Growing up with a fascination for celebrities, posters of his favorite pop stars lined the bedroom walls, where he spent hours gazing and fantasizing about their greatness. For Ramon, they were larger than life. Although now a grown man, with adult children and married to a wife who did not share his fantastical musings, Ramon continued to ponder the connection between his religious beliefs and cultural icons.

As the Sunday school teacher continued to rehearse the theological foundations of the resurrection of Jesus, something unique emerged into Ramon's consciousness. At first, he was frightened by the thought, but then he slowly allowed the vision to come to clarity within the frontal cortex of his brain.

Jesus Christ.

Elvis Presley.

Michael Jackson.

Ramon pondered as he explored the interrelatedness of these three pop icons. Briefly, his mind recalled the 1970 rock opera and musical *Jesus Christ Superstar*, an exploration of the psychological struggles of Jesus during the last days leading up to his crucifixion.

Thinking about the religious, cultural, and mythological themes drove Ramon's imagination to entertain a near blasphemous idea: "What if?" There was that question!

What if the historical Jesus in the Bible was just a famous actor instead of God's son sent to save us from our sins?

Ramon gasped internally at the very thought of such heresy. But he could not contain himself.

When Elvis and MJ died, obsessed fans began reporting sightings of them as if they had been raised from the dead, he recalled. The thought forced itself further into his mind.

What if every culture deals with the loss of its icons by fantasizing about their resurrection? What if resurrection is a natural cultural phenomenon that allows us to continue to have hope for the future?

As Ramon continued to reminisce, to the point of being oblivious to the Sunday school teacher's words, he suddenly remembered a documentary based on so-called Elvis sightings. The memory made him consider even more seriously the roots of cultural icons. Could it be that all cultures attempt to sustain their futures through the mythology of resurrection? If so, belief in the resurrection of Jesus is a theological and historical argument and a means for social survival.

Hero-mythology, whether in the movies or story form, gives us hope that if the hero survives death, we will all survive it. Or, does our denial of death keep us from embracing death as a natural extension of life?

These ideas and thoughts continued to penetrate the veneer of Ramon's otherwise conservative belief system as he continued to sit in the small classroom, with just enough space for fifteen people. But the thoughts and ideas flowing through Ramon could be catastrophic for all of Christendom. Or would it?

The Bible is not merely the words of God, but a book written by men with power-seeking motives looking to define culture in such a way as to serve and maintain its authority.

Ramon's thoughts are blasphemous and heretical at best.

What if?

That question again! Ramon could not stop it. The possibility of Jesus being this pop star of the first century who performed public dramas in the town's square to make social and political commentary about the ruling government intrigued him. No doubt such radicalism would get him crucified. But Ramon wondered, *What if instead of an actual historical event, the crucifixion and resurrection were acts in a theatrical performance designed to criticize the absurdity of Roman rule?*

Floods of ideas and thoughts swept through Ramon's imagination, making it difficult to pay attention to the Sunday school teacher. But more than a mental disruption, the view of Jesus as a Pop Idol Superstar who evolves into a folk legend and then emerges as a mythological character with divine traits created a subtle faith crisis for Ramon. Could such a thing be possible?

As a teacher of science, Ramon had always repudiated any revisionist hermeneutical models of history. However, he could not easily dismiss such a humanistic view of Jesus. Then, there was another dilemma. Who could he discuss these ideas with? Certainly not the pastor or Sunday school teacher, and not even his beloved wife would understand such an unimaginable deviation from doctrinal orthodoxy, so for the time being the thoughts were kept secret and buried in his conscious mind. He thought.

To believe or even entertain the idea of Jesus as anything other than God's holy Son had profound implications that Ramon had not yet calculated. Would it mean total devastation of his Christian identity? Since childhood, Ramon had been a believer in Jesus, in the Bible, and a regular church attendee. When most of his college friends strayed away from their upbringing's religious practices, Ramon seemed to reinforce them in his life.

Every decision Ramon had made revolved around his Christian devotion and practice: wife, career, where to attend college, live, attend church, and so on. Not being a Christian had never seemed like an option. To believe Jesus to be something other than the resurrected Lord had never occurred to him before. Theologically, one must ask the question: Does following Jesus require belief in him as a divine, all-powerful, all-knowing, resurrected being?

Despite the Sunday school teacher's voice echoing in the background, Ramon continued with his internal mental dialogue.

What is the real meaning of resurrection?

Is it a historical event or an existential reality?

Is it a state of being?

"Ramon." The Sunday school teacher's voice suddenly came crashing through his mental defenses. "You have been quiet today. Is there anything you want to add to the discussion?" the teacher asked.

It was apparent on Ramon's face that the Sunday school teacher's intrusion into his thoughts caught him by surprise. He stumbled for a moment and hesitantly considered framing a question that would reveal something about his heretical ruminations. But he stopped himself and decided not to disclose his radical ideas to the group.

"No, I am just glad it's Sunday," Ramon said.

Chapter 1

Prodigal

"You just don't understand," Yeshua screamed as he walked outside the family's home into the hot Galilean sun.

Yeshua's statement represented one out of a series of arguments with his father, Samuel, over issues related to family traditions and God's expectations. Their village, Gadara, was growing as commerce and trade increased. At sixteen, Yeshua had always been an independent spirit and *tekton* by trade. He taught himself how to build things and lay bricks, and was widely known for his masonry and carpentry skills in the surrounding villages. Since his birth, his relationship with his father had been strained and plagued by various peculiarities.

At times, the distance between them made it appear as if Samuel was not his birth father, a thought that frequently ran through Yeshua's mind.

Why did God make us so different?, Yeshua often thought. The plain truth of the matter was this: Yeshua was both embarrassed and intimidated by his father.

Samuel made his living as a pig farmer, something he learned to do early in life. He had moved the family away from Nazareth to escape public humiliation since there was nothing the locals despised more than a pig farmer. However, Samuel was no ordinary pig farmer. He regularly sold and exported swine meats at the markets by the sea. His fresh meats were in great demand among the more gentile neighbors. Swine and pork were considered a delicacy for the wealthy and social elites.

Samuel's meats were bought and sold throughout the empire as favorites at special events and meals. But few people knew of Samuel's agricultural wealth. He made it a point of living modestly in the village. He used his farm income to purchase land in the nearby towns and rented the land to other conventional farmers. His wealth over the years grew as tenant farmers became more and more in debt to him. Samuel understood the significance of land ownership over mere economic commodities.

Yeshua often wondered why Samuel chose such a deplorable way of life, but had never dared to ask. Samuel was rarely one to speak of his past with his chidren.

"When you get older, you will understand why I do what I do," Samuel yelled at Yeshua as he continued down the long path leading from their home to the main road that passed down the middle of the village. It was a road usually full of other travelers, both local and foreign. Their town was the largest concentration of dwellers before reaching the coastal lands close to the markets.

Yeshua continued walking, never acknowledging his father's cries, seemingly focused on getting started with his day. But he was listening. His father's voice pierced his consciousness and touched something shameful inside of him. It was a feeling he often felt, but as a Judean, he never understood. Samuel knew he was listening. He knew that his rants were embarrassing as the strangers walked by their house and could hear Samuel's pronouncements.

"You think you are too important to listen to your old father. But one day, you will realize. Just don't let it be too late," Samuel continued, a last desperate attempt to capture his son's attention.

Any response would have been satisfying. Both father and son stubbornly held their positions. They were two insatiable personalities stuck in a single-family drama, each refusing to change roles.

And so, Samuel continued, "I know where you are going, and I know what you have been up to. You better be careful. The emperor has no patience with such foolishness."

These words struck a nerve in Yeshua.

Is it true? Does he know? No way, Yeshua thought to himself as he finally reached the road in front of their house.

He picked up his pace and soon was out of sight of his father's house. People could now stop staring, stop whispering, and stop wondering why a father would be angry with his son. Yeshua was relieved to put some distance between himself and the pig farmer, wishing it was possible never to return.

But Yeshua depended on his father's generosity for his livelihood and self-understanding. In his world, a person was nothing without their family.

To ask for one's inheritance before the death of the father was inconceivable by Judean laws and customs. Samuel was in no mood to consider such an absurd request, and thus squander his fortune. And Yeshua was in no frame of mind to beg from a man who made his living among the filthy animals. So Yeshua just kept walking.

Instead of his father, Yeshua clung mostly to his mother. Even as an infant, he resisted any attempt to be weaned from her breast. His desperation to hold so tightly to Miriam gave him the official title among his brothers, "mama's boy."

But none of this bothered Miriam. As a daughter of Aaron ben Yuda, the wealthiest landowner in the region, being spoiled and held closely by one's parents was nothing new to her. Therefore, Yeshua's attachment seemed normal despite the traditional rites of passage ceremonies when boys became men and followed in their fathers' footsteps. Miriam supported her son's refusals to conform to the conventions of their customs and religions.

As in her upbringing, Miriam also was an independent spirit, particularly for a woman. She dared to claim to hear God's voice and often listened to the Spirit's leading, many times to the embarrassment of her father. Although many friends and family questioned their beloved neighbor's daughter's actions, few dared to speak directly to him about their sentiments.

"Why are you shouting so loud?" Miriam inquired as she greeted Samuel after he returned to their house. "It doesn't do any good for you to argue with him."

The intermediary role between Samuel and Yeshua was something Miriam observed early in life from her mother and father's relationship. At times she appeared to be too protective of Yeshua, something Samuel complained about.

"You need to let the boy be a man," he often said to her.

"I know, but he can only be a man when he knows that his father supports him and believes in him," she rebutted.

"What about me?" Samuel barked back. "Who believed in me? My father never supported me. Everything I gained I did for myself. There was no one to encourage me to be who I wanted to be. In the old days, you had to learn to take care of yourself and to take advantage of the opportunities that were in front of you."

Miriam knew that the argument with Samuel was useless but necessary for him to feel heard. It seemed that the only way Samuel knew how to express his feelings was through arguing against another point of view. Intuitively Miriam knew this about him and, far too many times, accommodated this dysfunction in him at the cost of her emotional well-being.

Ever since the oldest children had moved out on their own, she had felt trapped in the peacemaker role between these two stubborn men. Miriam worried a lot about the consequences of the divide between Samuel and Yeshua. Like her husband Samuel, she held close to their traditional values while reluctantly supporting Yeshua's dreams of being a street performer. Samuel's hard work, ingenuity, and faithfulness to God were the things that had sustained them over the years and enabled them to live a standard way of life, like the one her father provided.

Nothing was more important to her than keeping peace in the family. It was her lot in life to be the one who held things together. But now, tensions between Samuel and Yeshua were starting to feel out of control and could not be contained within the comforting walls of their household. Forces were brewing on the outside that could potentially mean disaster for them.

Meantime, Samuel settled for the status quo of life on the farm. He could not afford to spend too much time worrying about the situation. He had a business to run, people counting on him, and other challenges to face. So, in the quiet space between work and home, Samuel took a moment to reflect and think.

God has been good to me. I will not allow Yeshua's problems to become my problems. I have a blessed life with a good wife and family. All that I need, Adonai has provided. I will not allow my son's rebellious ways to waste all that I have worked for, he said to himself as the thoughts continued to occupy his mind.

LIKE FATHER, LIKE SON

The exchange with Yeshua triggered Samuel's memory of events that occurred thirty years ago when he too was a rebellious son and squandered his inheritance, which resulted in his unconventional and illegitimate marriage to Miriam. As he stood in the doorway of his home, gazing at Yeshua as he slowly disappeared in the distance, he daydreamed about the years leading to the day when he finally decided to visit his father to make amends for the past. Although their marriage consummated without the customary parental transactions, Samuel was determined to right the wrongs of his past.

Samuel often felt alone around his own family. He grew up in the town of Shechem, the youngest of nine children. Samuel saw himself in Yeshua. He, too, was once the rebellious son who refused to comply with his father's hopes and dreams. At the age of twelve, he came to his father and asked for the total of his inheritance.[1] Such a request was unprecedented prior to a father's death. Samuel had since carried with him the guilt for the way

---

1. Luke 15:11–32.

he treated his father, but the city's appeal caused Samuel to often dream of making it on his own in a new place. So, he set out on foot to Nazareth.

Once on his own in the city, hard times fell on Samuel. He squandered his inheritance, hanging out late at night in the town with friends. Friends always come easy when you have the resources to pay for everyone's needs. Samuel's friends were no different. But when hard times came, and the resource pool dried up, Samuel found himself alone.

To make ends meet, he found work attending swine for a Greek farmer. It was considered the lowest of occupations for any of his people. But Samuel was desperate and determined not to return home to face his father's disappointment.

Although times were difficult and Samuel missed the comforts of home and the innocence of his protective existence, he grew as a person and learned a lot about life. Pious, the owner, a Greek merchant, generously shared with Samuel. He taught him many things about the farming and trade businesses. Despite their cultural and ethnic differences, Pious learned to see Samuel as another son. He shared ideas about owning a business, managing your earnings, and saving for the days of famine.

The three years spent working on the farm seemed to go by fast. As Samuel grew into adulthood, he had dreams of starting his own business. By then he had acquired skills in carpentry and woodworking. Living in a city near the sea afforded him many opportunities to learn about trade, speaking multiple languages, and interacting with diverse cultures.

The most significant occurrence was meeting Miriam. She was the daughter of a wealthy landowner from Tyre, and the only female of six children who made their living growing wheat and fruit. Samuel first met Miriam while perusing the market on a late afternoon before the beginning of Sabbath. Their first meeting was awkward, mostly smiles and long glances at each other. Finally, Samuel mustered enough courage to ask her for a drink of water from one of the pots near her fruit stand.

Knowing the social and historical connotations of such a request, Miriam immediately felt delighted to be wooed by Samuel's premarital proposal. After a series of encounters over three months, her parents made plans for their betrothal. But Samuel had some unfinished business before consummating their marriage. Adonai would not accept his marriage to Miriam without the blessings of his father. So, he set his sights on the three-day journey toward his father's home. The thought of reconciling with his father consumed Samuel. He had to find a way to restore his honor and trust. His older brothers, who had stayed home and followed the family's tradition of working faithfully on his father's farm, would no doubt despise Samuel for the way he disgraced his father's honor. What would he say? What would he do? How would he be treated? As a stranger? Friend? Enemy? Who alone but God knew?

But it had to be done.

"I know what I must do," Samuel said to Miriam as he continued to pack his bags for the journey to his father's farm. "I have been the prodigal for too long. I will present myself as my father's servant and work for him until I have repaid my debt to him."

Miriam knew better than trying to talk him out of it. A long time ago, she learned that no word or deed could change Samuel's mind when he wanted to do something. At times, his stubbornness frustrated Miriam, but his commitment to traditional values and ideals also attracted her to him.

As the oldest, Miriam grew up accustomed to deferring to the authority of men. Her father, Aaron, was also a robust authoritarian personality. Her mother, Ruth, often subjugated herself, and her children, to her husband's irrational religious demands. Miriam, too, was shaped by the same culture of obedience and submission.

The price for such loyalty was difficult to measure. On the one hand, Samuel, ten years her senior, provided shelter and protection in an otherwise hostile environment where women and children were mere property. Although a man of principle, Samuel showed little passion or love for Miriam. However, his devotion to her and the family was simply a matter of duty. To do otherwise would be considered a social disgrace. Miriam understood Samuel and the world that birthed him. At the same time, she carried around inside her a longing for something more, something different, something self-affirming.

"Let me help you," Miriam insisted as Samuel fumbled in the dark, looking for the essentials of his journey.

It was no surprise to him to hear Miriam offer her assistance. It had been their routine since their marriage consummated. Samuel had become adept at pretending to be lost, only to be rescued by Miriam, even as he protested her intrusion. Pride demanded that he appear independent and self-sufficient. Miriam colluded with her husband's pride as any "good" wife would do. Little did Samuel know that Miriam had been planning for his leave since early that morning.

"This should do it," Miriam stated with confidence, having cooked his meals for three days, washed extra clothes, packed a blanket for the cold nights, and filled his water container.

Miriam overlooked no detail as she empathized with the emotional burden that her husband carried inside him every day of their marriage. It was always written on his face, evident in his posture, and influenced almost every decision. She was fully aware that she had married a man of principle and deep convictions.

Samuel would never be the husband she wanted him to be until he faced his father's wrath. No priest could help him—only an understanding and supportive wife. So, they both closed their eyes and went to sleep before rising early for the next day's journey.

THE STREET PERFORMER

Yeshua had always been different from most Judean men, and there were times when he wished he had settled for conventional norms. Without knowing his father's past, he could not see just how much he was like Samuel, and consequently, his uniqueness sometimes made him feel lonely. No one seemed to understand who he was and what he wanted to accomplish through his work.

Many thought his passion for street performing was the negative influence of Roman ideas on a child's education, a conclusion with few merits considering that most parents could not afford to send their children to the synagogues. Rabbinical teachings exclusively came from the stories in the Talmud.

Yeshua first fell in love with drama when his class performed a reenactment of Moses and the Egyptians. Rabbi Tendell wrote the main piece and quickly recognized Yeshua's giftedness for performance art. Although the theatre was a populist invention of the Greeks and the Romans, the synagogue curriculum also included the repetitive rehearsal of those moments in history when God saved the people.

Most educated people held some awareness of the Greek actor, Thespis, who toured around the ancient world performing narratives that commonly became known as Greek Tragedies. Actors assumed the role of some famous person and performed speeches with their faces hidden behind masks. Stories about Thespis and his impact on the political landscape were legendary.

Although Yeshua spent several months as a tekton apprentice, financed by his father, he had no formal education in the universities. His unusual appreciation for the art of dramatic performing and its radical potential came from his friendships with several academy students who followed the Thespisic traditions. Several of them faced brutal repercussions by the current ruling administration's intolerance of any subversive activity that threatened or ridiculed its authority. Dramas involving political satire were discouraged and ran the risk of imprisonment or even execution. Ironically, it became the form of acting that attracted Yeshua the most.

However, it was not his only attraction.

Chapter 2

Prodigy

ALEXIA, THE DAUGHTER OF a wealthy aristocrat of indigenous Egyptian royalty, was the by-product of Greco-Roman acculturation. Her mother was the daughter of Judean landowners from the south. Intelligent and very well educated in both Judean and Greek culture, she was the youngest of five children, and the only daughter. She often felt competitive with her older brothers, although they seldom spent time together. They shared only the same father, and Alexia was the center of his affections. Luke and Cephus, the younger sons, lived in their father's residence with Alexia. The older sons, Joel and Simeon, lived in the town of Cephas with their mother.

Yeshua and Alexia had several small encounters while he worked on various masonry projects for Alexia's father around their compound. Yeshua's skills at sculpting detailed images of human bodies and ornamental objects on the sides of buildings and palace walls made him a favorite tekton in the region. Most conversations between Alexia and Yeshua were brief and awkward at first, but over time, as Yeshua became more fluent in Greek, they learned to speak in more familiar terms.

Yeshua's most recent encounter with Alexia happened when they were both young teenagers. With Yeshua's brother James's assistance, the government commissioned Yeshua to build a new wall around the back terrace. Yeshua did most of the masonry work, showcasing his mastery of laying a plumb line while sneaking glimpses at the beautiful Alexia.

"I think your father is looking for you," Alexia said one afternoon while sitting on the back terrace.

These were her first words to Yeshua. He was finishing a row of bricks on the wall next to the side of the house where Alexia usually practiced her music lessons. Yeshua was delighted to have the chance to interact with her.

"Thank you for telling me. But I do not know where to find him," Yeshua said. Not knowing anything else to say to keep her attention. "Shall I look for him?"

"That will not be necessary. I will let your father know where you are," she said. "By the way, what is your name?"

Yeshua had been waiting for this moment, so he quickly seized the opportunity for more conversation.

"My family name is Yeshua. But most people know me as Yason," he said. "So, call me Yason."

Alexia smiled and seemed to welcome Yeshua's invitation. Although they grew up only a few miles apart, the cultural divide between them was wide and steep in tradition. But something more significant than their differences was about to bring them together in unimaginable ways.

It was Alexia whom Yeshua first trusted to tell about his love of theatre. Alexia was always supportive and shared Yeshua's interest in the arts. She promised to come see one of his performances but had to wait for her father's permission.

Finally, when Alexia turned sixteen, her father granted permission to see one of Yeshua's street performances as a birthday gift. Accompanied by escorts, she attended a performance near their palace.

Yeshua performed solo in the role of a young Judean boy who had intentionally tried to escape his parents' oversight while visiting the city to pay their annual taxes.[1] The boy took refuge in the synagogue during the mid-day discussions among the Rabbis. Everyone attending was astounded by the maturity and wisdom of the questions posed by the boy. His knowledge and wisdom confounded the elders.

"That was really good," said Alexia.

Yeshua, having just descended from the platform where he performed, turned around.

"Thank you very much for saying so. I have never seen you here before," as he smiled and gazed into her eyes, intentionally wanting her to know that she, and only she, had captured his attention.

His radiant smile disclosed a perfect set of brilliant white teeth, arranged in his mouth as if they were designed specifically by the creator. Her heart began to beat faster in response to his smile, permitting him to press forward with the introduction.

1. Luke 2:41.

I must not let her know how much I want her company, Yeshua thought as he planned his next move.

"I don't usually come to these parts," Alexia began, "but I have heard so much about your performances and wanted to see for myself."

Alexia stood mesmerized by his sheer display of self-confidence. It was almost as if Yeshua had grown up and turned into a man overnight. Or maybe she was turning into a woman? *What a specimen of a man*, she thought as her eyes surveyed the bronzed, six-foot-three frame of a man who appeared to be much older than the part he had just played. Yeshua's dark skin, long curly hair, and muscular physique were more than her eyes could contain. It took almost every fiber of her being to maintain a poised disposition, to keep him from noticing the effect his presence was having on her.

"I am glad you did. You must come more often," Yeshua responded quickly, careful not to prematurely reveal his true intentions.

Being a street performer, Yeshua was conditioned to hide and mask his true feelings, something that would prove to be both a blessing and a curse to him. But Alexia could see beyond the veiled expression on his face. She knew exactly what he was up to and was delighted to be the object of his attraction.

Playing along, Alexia responded, "Perhaps I will if I know when you are performing again?"

Alexia's invitation did not go unnoticed by Yeshua, who quickly seized upon the opportunity to invite her to his next performance. But this performance would be special, not on the crowded streets, but privately as they got to know each other over the coming seasons.

SIX MONTHS LATER

"It seems like we have known each other forever," Alexia said as they walked along the road leading from the sea. "You seem to know what I am going to say before it ever comes out of my mouth."

Each town and village were connected by roads and waterways. Yeshua traveled them most of his life with Samuel as they transported swine meats to markets. He hoped the casual setting would be the perfect way to learn more about Alexia. Only a few travelers were on the road today. The sun sat low in the eastern sky as a gentle breeze cooled the heat on their faces. Few people took the path since it was often occupied with caravans of livestock. Alexia's guardians walked closely behind them to ensure her safety.

Alexia continued, "I am looking forward to seeing another one of your performances in a few days."

"Thank you for agreeing to come. I hope it doesn't disappoint you," Yeshua said.

"It will do no such thing. You have a brilliant mind," Alexia smiled.

"Thank you again. How do you know such things?" Yeshua asked.

"Because I just do," Alexia laughed. "I have listened to many philosophers and religious thinkers most of my life. Some of them are friends of my father and often came to our home for the afternoon meals. I have learned to tell the difference between an intellectual and a fool. You are not a fool."

"You know so many things to be such a young woman," Yeshua said to keep Alexia talking about herself. "How is it so?"

"I had many good tutors growing up as the daughter of a Roman official. As the only female, I spent much of my time in the home where I learned to read and write. Evening meals were often discussions about Rome and my father's interests in culture. I learned early how to listen well and not be noticed among men. You can learn a lot about a person just by listening to them."

Alexia paused, hoping to get a chance to shift the conversation back to Yeshua. She liked talking endlessly at times and was afraid she would talk too much.

"So, what is your favorite subject?" asked Yeshua.

Abandoning her plans to shift the conversation back to Yeshua, Alexia responded without hesitation. "Definitely politics. My father named me after the great Alexander, so I have always felt a lure toward political matters."

"That's interesting," said Yeshua. "What political issues interest you the most?"

"I am embarrassed to say." She looked down, noticed the footprints of sheep, which must have been the last kind of animal to be led down the dusty road.

"Don't feel ashamed. I will not judge you," said Yeshua as he waited for Alexia to speak, hoping he would be able to contain his instincts.

"I believe women should have more rights in our city. Many of us are as enlightened as men, but we don't have a right to speak our minds in public," Alexia said with an expression of caution on her face, wondering if she had revealed too much.

"You are a fascinating woman with interesting ideas. Where did these strange ideas come from?" Yeshua inquired.

"I once had a tutor from Athens who spoke about a concept called democratic participation. She said that in Athens there are frequent discussions about a future society where women and men will be equals, elections will be held to select government leaders, and people will be free to share their thoughts openly in the public square. It all seemed too idealistic at the time. But as I get older it is starting to make sense to me." Alexia was now feeling more relaxed and excited to share these ideas with someone. "Do you think I am mad to have these ideas?"

Yeshua quickly responded, "Not at all. Your ideas are reasonable, though we may never see such a thing in our lifetime. Even the ancient prophets spoke about a new covenant among the people. I am sure they meant women too."

"Thank you, Yason, for listening to my ideas," Alexia said while looking up again into his blueish-green eyes. "I really enjoy talking and walking with you. There is something so different about you."

"I feel the same about you. Although our worlds are far apart from each other, there is a bond I feel between us," Yeshua said.

"I feel it too," said Alexia as they embraced.

Galilee was within their sights now. They had only a few more moments together before parting ways so as not to be seen together by the locals. News traveled slowly in rural areas. They both were aware that news about a Judean peasant and the daughter of a Roman official would eventually make its way into every village and town in the region.

The relationship between Yeshua and Alexia seemed to blossom over the coming months as they spent more time together. But brewing underneath their love for each other were the cold realities that would shake the foundation of their newfound romance. Amid their common admiration were the inherent differences imposed upon them by cultural and historical realities beyond their control. Yeshua was the son of a Judean landowner. Alexia was the daughter of an aristocrat. Yeshua was less sophisticated than Alexia, a relatively poor, uneducated street performer who criticized and antagonized the governmental leadership. Alexia lived in a palace, under the watchful eye of her father's servants and was born in an elitist family influenced by Greek and Roman culture.

Their two worlds were never meant to coexist.

THE SECRET

Most of Alexia's days were spent completing studies at the Alexandrian school of literature. Roman citizenship gave her tremendous freedoms, although she remained under constant guardianship. Occasionally, Alexia traveled to Cephas to see her older brothers and visit her favorite cousin, Elizabeth.

It took over half a day to journey to Damascus by foot. It would have taken longer except for the special permissions to pass through security checkpoints. Alexia was seldom out of the view of employed escorts.

Spending time with her cousin was particularly important. Elizabeth was some years older than Alexia and consequently was more like a big sister or surrogate mother. It was getting late into spring and the evenings were getting warmer.

On this visit, Alexia planned to spend the Sabbath in Elizabeth's home with her husband, Zechariah, an administrative assistant to the governor in Galilee. The governor provided a modest home for Elizabeth and her husband. It had plenty of room to accommodate Alexia for the Sabbath.

As her entourage approached the small home, Elizabeth stood in the pathway waiting on Alexia's arrival. The excitement on her face was a clear reflection of the anticipation in her heart. Alexia, with a smile on her face, embraced Elizabeth.

"You are blessed among women," Elizabeth said as they both broke out in laughter.[2]

The phrase was a part of their usual greeting, partly because of the adoration they felt for each other, and partly for the comedic idea that either one of them would claim such a status.

Alexia did not immediately respond, but paraded around Elizabeth, raising her head and pretending to be a blessed woman.

"Thank you, cousin, for your generous words. But you and I both know that I am not that woman, nor do I wish to be." Both women joined in laughter.

"Cousin, you are who you are. That's why I love you so much," said Elizabeth. This interchange was nothing new. They had rehearsed it many times.

Alexia spoke softly in Elizabeth's ear, "You, on the other hand, should be highly favored for the life you tolerate every day."

They refrained from hugging, looked into each other's eyes, and continued holding hands as in a moment of quiet desperation. They both knew the secret truth and the pain between them, that Elizabeth was not treated well by her husband, Zechariah. But talking about him would be a waste of their time.

"Alexia, look at you. You are beaming in a way that I have never seen before," Elizabeth exclaims.

"It is the Sabbath, cousin. We should all be rejoicing for this time of rest and reflection," Alexia says.

2. Luke 1:42.

"I agree, cousin. But as one woman to another, I know that look on your face. Who is he? What is his name? Is he rich?" Elizabeth probed.

"I do not know what you are talking about, Elizabeth," Alexia said, as she walked away toward the path leading to the home.

"Is he rich? Does he own land? Is he a citizen of Rome? I always prayed that you would marry someone who loved and honored you." Elizabeth said, not knowing the full impact of her words.

The insinuation proved to be effective in seducing Alexia to reveal her secret. She reached down and pulled Elizabeth's arm toward her as they scurried to the adjacent field next to the house, far away from Zechariah's ear.

Upon arrival, Alexia breathed deeply, anxious about what she was about to reveal to the most trusted person in her life. The field of wheat was in the middle of the harvest but provided adequate cover from any suspecting bystanders. Two guardians followed them, but said nothing.

"What I am about to tell, you must not tell anyone," Alexia whispered as she looked at Elizabeth.

"Alexia, you can trust me. I swear on my life," Elizabeth assured her.

"Yes, I have met a man. He is not like any man I have ever met before. He is tall, dark, and wise beyond his years. We have so much in common. Cousin, I think he may be the one if Adonai says so," Alexia said.

Elizabeth reached to embrace Alexia. "Truly you are highly favored among women," she said. "Who is this man? A roman official or a Greek god?"

"No. He is neither. He is a Judean but grew up near Nazareth. He is a street performer for a group called The Ekklesia. His vision for a new world is so amazing. We talk all the time about what it will mean for all people."

Elizabeth interrupted. "Are you talking about Yeshua?"

"Why yes," Alexia responded, surprised.

"People have been talking about his performances. They have been drawing enormous crowds which have caused Rome to be a little nervous. Is he rich?" Elizabeth asked with a bit of sarcasm.

"His father owns a lot of farmland if you must know. But Yeshua is like me: he has a passion for the simple and profound, and does not allow any amount of denarii to determine his thoughts," Alexia explained.

"I love you, Alexia, like a sister. If you are happy, I am happy. This man must be something special for you to take such a risk. You know as well as I do what your father would say about his daughter being with a common Judean. Please be careful about your relationship with this man. Take your time and do not rush things until you are sure you love him enough to lose all you have," Elizabeth said as she reached to embrace Alexia.

"Don't worry. I will be careful," Alexia said.

Not only did the relationship between Yeshua and Alexia grow over time, but the popularity of The Ekklesia also expanded exponentially over the next three years. The crowds were now numbering in the hundreds and the appeal was diversifying. A new movement was beginning and transforming everything as it had been known.

Over time, Alexia became more concerned about the disparities in their backgrounds though Yeshua seemed not to notice. At times his obliviousness worried her. She was never quite sure how to bring up the subject for discussion, not wanting to interrupt the pleasant sensation of the love between them. But at night, when they were at home in their separate abodes, she could not push the thoughts out of her mind about the inherent differences surrounding their relationship. She felt torn between her loyalty to the family's reputation and her love for Yeshua, who had opened her eyes to new truths about the world.

Navigating between worlds had been Alexia's existence since childhood. Being the daughter of a Roman official gave her both privilege and anonymity. For the most part, her identity was often eclipsed by the celebrity status of her parents. Still seen as too young to be married, her status remained dormant in the eyes of most people. Therefore, she was often able to move around from one part of the providence to the other without being noticed. Since women usually wore traditional clothing, Alexia typically dressed modestly, even to the point of occasionally wearing a veil. But she was in no way under obligation to conform to the Halacha standards. One of the advantages of class status is that people are afforded more options outside orthodoxy.

A WOMAN AT THE WELL

One day while Yeshua was alone rehearsing his lines, Alexia quietly walked up behind him and covered his eyes with her hands. She did not have to say anything. He immediately recognized the soft touch of her breasts pressed against the middle of his spine. Without hesitation, he grabbed her hands and pulled them down below his waist touching the inside of his thigh. Knowing that she had been discovered her hands quickly relaxed and relinquished their control.

Yeshua then turned around, "What a pleasant surprise. I was not expecting you today. But I am glad you are here. Where are your guardians?"

"My father was summoned to the emperor's palace and had to leave. So, he canceled our afternoon family discussions about politics and philosophy.

As soon as his chariot left, I rushed out of the side gate without my guardians' knowledge," Alexia explained. "Am I interrupting something?"

"No, I was going over the next performance," Yeshua said.

"Well, I won't keep you from your work," Alexia responded.

"You are not disturbing me at all." Yeshua said, before thinking of a clever way to keep her from leaving. "Would you like to hear about it?"

"I would love to," Alexia smiled at the invitation.

"It is about a woman from Samaria who comes to Jacob's well to draw water.[3] She does this every day, usually at the hottest time of the day when she knows the other women are not around," Yeshua said with excitement in his voice.

"Are Samaritans welcome in those parts?" Alexia asked.

"No, they are not. That is exactly why I am telling this story. It is these divisions among the people that oppress us," Yeshua said.

"Tell me more," Alexia said, sitting down at Yeshua's feet.

"Every day this woman makes the long journey to fill her water pot and returns to her village. But one day she comes, and a strange man is sitting there on the edge of the well. She is stunned to see a Judean man. She is frightened, not truly knowing what his intentions are. She has never seen a man at the well before. She thinks to herself, 'Should I run away?' But her family depends on her for water. Before she can decide, the man says to her, 'Woman, give me a drink.'" Yeshua paused.

Alexia shouted, "Really? Is that not the traditional way to make a marriage proposal?"

Yeshua said, "Yes. That's what she thinks. But she is confused. He is Judean and she is Samaritan. It is forbidden for them to marry. Besides, she has been proposed to many times before by men who have abandoned her. She doesn't know if she can trust another man."

"So, what happens next?" Alexia asked.

"The stranger sees the look on her face and knows what she is feeling inside. He assures her that if she accepts his proposal, he will never abandon her. He promises to take care of her and her family," Yeshua explained.

"But what about their differences?" Alexia inquired.

"Love knows no boundaries," Yeshua said, staring directly into Alexia's eyes. Suddenly it occurred to her that the story was about them. Her heart sank.

"So, Yason, who will be this woman?" Alexia asked, pretending to be jealous. "Will she be beautiful and young?"

---

3. John 4:4–26.

"Yes, she must be beautiful beyond imagination," Yeshua responded knowingly in order to incite Alexia's jealous feelings. "I know just the right person to perform this role."

"Who is she?" Alexia asked, burning with jealousy.

"You!" Yeshua said.

"What? You are making a mockery of me," Alexia said, not finding Yeshua's humor amusing. It now occurred to her what Yeshua was talking about.

Up until now, she had remained in the background of his performances, content with her supportive role and encouraging him. Besides, her father must never know about their love. Being in one of Yeshua's performances was more than she could imagine. If she was caught participating in Yeshua's plot to subvert the Roman rule, she would likely be disowned by her father and suffer the same fate as the others. Images portraying all the possible outcomes raced through her mind as Yeshua continued to insist on her involvement. But the truth of the matter was this—she was already caught up in his drama.

I am the Samaritan woman, Alexia thought to herself but continued to play along.

"In this drama, the Judean man will propose to this woman," Yeshua continued. "She will accept his proposal and return to her village to let the elders know about the marriage. But her father will forbid marriage between a Judean and a Samaritan. So, the entire village will run to the well to see this man and tell him to leave their land. But the woman will run to warn him that her father and the people intend to kill him if he doesn't leave. When she tries to warn him, he will beg her to run away with him. He will promise to take her to a place where she will never thirst or want ever again. She will not be able to resist his invitation. So, they will both run away together and live in peace for the rest of their lives."

Realizing the deeper meaning of Yeshua's words, Alexia spoke without pretense, "Yes, I will be in your performance and in your life. I promise to be with you when the time comes. I will never leave your side. I will love you forever and I will always be yours."

Yeshua pulled Alexia close to him as he pressed his lips against hers. "And I will always be yours," he said, barely able to speak the words between each kiss.

Chapter 3

Disciples

Yᴇsʜᴜᴀ's sᴜᴄᴄᴇss ᴀs ᴀ street performer did not occur overnight. It came with much sacrifice, joy, and resistance over the years. At the age of twenty-five, he was considered one of the most popular actors in the province. Initially, he performed as a solo artist, making spontaneous appearances wherever a crowd gathered. Reading the masses was something he learned to do instinctively. It was a necessary skill to survive in the market-driven conditions of Palestine. Groups of people, usually over a hundred, helped signal the presence of many things. Either they represented the presence of food, money, or trouble. Yeshua was always mindful that crowds both saved you and protected you from the power of the government.

THE CROWDS

But crowds often possessed their unique personalities. Gaining the crowd's attention and respect was something that came and went in an instant. Often acting as an independent enity, the crowd's temperment could determine the success or failure of a performance. Crowds could be moody, hungry, frightened, nervous, excited, temperamental, and any other characteristic of a single human being. Yeshua by now had become adept at reading the crowds, knowing when to engage with them and when to simply leave them alone for another day.

Since he was not allowed to perform in Rome's arenas, Yeshua relied on more unconventional venues for his dramas, such as street corners, markets, and small house gatherings. Merging the two popular genres of tragedy and comedy into one cohesive theatrical display showed his real genius as a street performer. Yeshua mastered the best of Euripides's provocative dialogues, often using his techniques to invoke the crowd's sympathy. Although his subject matter was less sophisticated than Greek philosophy, his ability to engage the audience's passions was equally as audacious as most Greek productions' stagings.

THE CASTS

Yeshua's unique ability to draw the crowd into a story, with his colorful monologues, filled with graphic metaphorical language, captured his fans' imagination. In addition to the use of other performers, Yeshua's ability to reenact various roles gave him a versatility few actors possessed. He could assume multiple famous and infamous leaders' personalities in his stories and was adept at performing both male and female characters. Most of the roles were familiar to him and his audience, usually members of the local government. The key was to make light of their significance while also offering satirical commentary. For the first few years, Yeshua switched characters around in each scene, often leaving the audience in suspense about the plot's direction.

As he matured in performing, and the plots became more complex, Yeshua added more actors to his company. Adding people involved expanding the parts of his narratives, making them longer, and making the plot development more complicated.

Rehearsals often took place late in the evening. Getting others to commit to a rigorous schedule of rehearsals and performances was not easy. Several joined and later deserted under the pressure of Yeshua's standards. After several failed attempts, Yeshua eventually established a cohort of faithful actors. They chose the name The Ekklesia to represent the special bond between them and to raise consciousness among the ordinary people. With no money to guarantee or incentivize prospective members, Yeshua attracted socially conscious actors who wanted to make a difference in the people's circumstances.

Petras was nearly ten years older than Yeshua, but passionate about acting. He had been married since the age of sixteen and lived with his wife and her sick mother. His interest came later in life after a career as a fisherman. One day, while unloading a boat near the seaport, he saw a crowd of people standing nearby at the fruit stands adjacent to the docks.

He was curious about what was drawing the attention of so many people. *I wish I could draw fish as plentiful as the people standing over there,* he said to himself as he wandered closer to see what was happening.

Seeing Yeshua's enactment of the healing of a blind man by the side of the road was so compelling, not to mention the symbolism of using spittle as salve, that Petras later asked Yeshua if he could study under him.[1]

"I want to learn this new art form, and to be something more than just a fisherman," Petras said to Yeshua. "I am the blind man! My life is without purpose—like a ship lost at sea. But now I see."

"Stay with me, and I will make you a fisher of men," Yeshua replied as he placed his hand on Petras's shoulder, assuring him that he would not regret his decision.

Yeremiah was the first to join Yeshua in his quest to transform Palestine and stir the peasant masses. They had the most in common. Both were poor, uneducated, and rebellious of their father's hopes and expectations. They both felt isolated from their families and believed they did not fit in. Yeremiah was the son of a temple custodian. He could not ever remember a time when he wanted to follow in his father's footsteps. He also came from a large family of ten children. His mother took exclusive responsibility for raising Yeremiah, his five sisters and four brothers.

Unlike Petras or Yeremiah, Matthew, educated in philosophy and the arts, was literate in both languages. He often taught Torah lessons at the temple and synagogues. Before joining the group, Matthew lectured at the Alexandria site called Mars Hill. He enjoyed the debates between Greek and Eastern philosophers. Since few scholars could read and write, Matthew was well respected among both elites and peasantry leaders. Over the years, his eyesight was getting worse, and now he had to hold papyri close to his face to read them.

Yohanan joined the group after having worked as a carpenter on many projects with Yeshua. They met a couple of years earlier, making wooden props for some of his dramas. As the quiet one in the group, acting gave him an outlet to help overcome his introversion.

For three years, Yael, one of the female members, played small roles in the street performances. She first joined The Ekklesia soon after turning twelve years old, mostly playing child's roles, both male and female. One recent character was a devout young woman who mysteriously became

---

1. John 9:1–33.

pregnant without the involvement of a husband.[2] The entire short act had only two scenes. Each focused on the religious and moral connotations of God rewarding her with a son without a human father. Yeshua intentionally chose not to reveal the name of the son. He wanted to leave the audience anticipating the unveiling of the character in a subsequent performance.

Yael's short frame suited the part well. Her thick brown hair and full lips provoked images of traditional Judean daughters. If her parents had the slightest knowledge of her participation in the street performances, it would mean the end of her acting career.

"The streets are no place for young girls," her mother once said. Yael's passion for street performing ran counter to the traditional belief that a woman's place was at home, learning to be a wife one day.

Others joined The Ekklesia as it grew in popularity. Some were support casts who helped with props and small complimentary parts. Marco and James (the brother of Yeshua) were responsible for staging the performances so the stories featured realistic backgrounds. Thomas joined the group later and offered a critical perspective to some of the narrative lines. The last to become a part of The Ekklesia was Judas. He had no experience acting but was a helpful handyman.

THE EMPIRE

As Yeshua's popularity grew, so did the anticipated curiosity of the new governor in Galilee. Simon was a generous governor, more than those who were appointed previously. He also was a man of principle. Simon made many sacrifices to gain favor from the emperor. His marginal participation in Judean life often was rewarded by the trust of the Roman hierarchy. His acquired wealth as a commercial trader allowed him to transcend many of the same lot's typical plight. As the husband of an Egyptian princess, Simon symbolized social achievement's apex while also being viewed as a prime example of religious heresy. Most people either hated or admired him.

By now, three things were apparent indicators of potential threats to Yeshua's leadership. First, the crowds enlarged in size after each performance by The Ekklesia. When the performances only attracted a random sampling of fifteen or so people, Rome paid less attention to Yeshua or the subject matter of his performances. As time passed, reports estimated crowds of two hundred or more. If efforts to regulate the audience's size were not made, major interruptions to other commercial industries could result. Often the people engrossed in the performances were the same people who bartered

2. Matt 1:18.

for products from the other vendors. The attention focused on Yeshua and his dramas was beginning to pose a threat to the economy.

Along with the crowds' size, there were concerns about critiquing the structures of the local government, though nothing, so far, had been too egregious. The previous week's performances appeared to offer more comic relief than radical disdain for the current administration.

But Rome was sensitive about matters that criticized its leaders. The emperor, Thaddeus, by most people's accounts, was a benevolent and generous ruler. Many would say he was the best Caesar Rome had ever seen, while others considered him a tyrant. For sure, Thaddeus of Belvar was a leader who demanded nothing less than complete loyalty from his subjects. He was the indisputable emperor, however, less religiously zealous and pompous than his predecessors.

At the young age of twenty, Thaddeus was also one of the youngest to rule. His military experience and vision were modestly ambitious. More notable had been his liberal tolerance of the Judean peasantry. He relied heavily on his cabinet administrators for the daily tasks of running the empire, appointing governors in the various provinces who shared some common cultural and religious heritage with the people. This strategy seemed to have proven wise on his part and impeded any rebellious uprisings.

Executions tended to be more sport for him than public deterrence. His greatest love was for the arts and humanities. He had built several libraries since the beginning of his rule. History would remember him as the domestic emperor, unlike his father, Julius, whose appetite for conquest and expansion left a bloody path through the annals of history.

No one dared to question Thaddeus's authority. Not even Petula. She was the first, and therefore the principal, wife and childhood companion. At times their relationship appeared more sibling-like than romantic. Some speculate that there was a good reason for the familiar tone of their marriage. As his favorite wife, Thaddeus trusted her more than any other person.

"You know people are beginning to talk," she said to Thaddeus as they relaxed on the upper porch overlooking the central pool, heavily fortified with columns and stone walls.

"Talking about what. . .us?" Thaddeus responded with a bit of sarcasm.

"No, you know what I am talking about," she responded. Petula was well acquainted with Thaddeus's tendency to avoid confrontation. "The crowds in the street," she said to rescue him from having to deal directly with the subject and even her. "The crowds are growing. Reports say they are the largest ever seen, mostly around the noonday."

Thaddeus still appeared reluctant to engage in the matter. "That is of no concern to me. Let the governor Simon deal with it," he said.

Petula was now annoyed and continued with the assertion. "That may be true, but others within the cabinet are getting nervous about the potential security risk," she said.

"Security risk!" Thaddeus chuckled at the idea. "These people are too concerned about appeasing their god than to anger me with any demonstration of disloyalty."

Petula softened her tone as she sipped more wine, "I understand, husband, but I don't think it is a good idea for one man to have that much attention."

"What man is that?" Thaddeus had not been paying attention to the daily reports from the cabinet.

Thaddeus's unawareness of the growing popularity of Yeshua's performances was indicative of his administrative style. However, one could not assume that he did not possess the same qualities as any of Rome's emperors. Pride, jealousy, insecurity, and anger all still ran deeply through his veins. No challenge or threat to his authority would go unnoticed. During a pregnant pause before Petula made her revelation of the man in the street, Thaddeus thought to himself.

> "What man is this? Things have been so quiet during my five
> years as supreme ruler. No one has ever questioned my authority.
> Is this the time when such a thing will happen? It has been the
> very thing I have feared the most. I have stayed awake many
> nights, anticipating a violent revolt in the middle of the night by
> some unexpected foe. Could this be the time? There were rumors
> of a resurgence last year, but it proved to be nothing. Am I ready
> for the test? A man can not know for sure how strong his power is
> until someone challenges it. Is this my time?"

His thoughts began to race at the speed of light as flashes of his demise displayed across the canvass of his consciousness. The idea of such a thing was more than he could bear.

"What is this man's name? Who is he?" Thaddeus finally asked.

"His name is Yeshua, son of Samuel," Petula answered. "He is a young peasant who puts on street theatre. Perhaps it is nothing to be concerned about for now," she assured her husband. "But some of the reports have been noticing the crowds are starting to increase in numbers. It started with about five to ten people, and now there are as many as two hundred at his performances."

Thaddeus seemed relieved yet still interested. "So, what are these dramas about?" he asked.

Petula could not answer specifically. She, like her husband, spent most of her existence secluded within their fortified palaces. She was only privy to brief reports from others who occasionally ventured out into the marketplace. The information was only second and thirdhand, no doubt embellished and intended to draw attention.

"I hear they are little funny stories about some of the well-known Judean leaders, mostly religious peasants," she said. "I don't think there is much to be concerned about, but it may not be a bad idea to remind the public that civil discord will not be tolerated."

Thaddeus nodded in agreement.

Petula continued, "You spend too much of your time away from the public view. People need to see you more often, know who you are and what you will or will not tolerate. It would not hurt to make an appearance soon to reassure the people of the strength of your leadership."

Thaddeus seemed convinced by her words.

"People love you, both Judean and Greek," Petula added. "But they need assurances that you also love them."

Thaddeus's expression on his face appeared to confirm the integrity of Petula's words. The choice of words was not one of his strengths. He considered himself an intellectual, but not a persuasive theoretician or public speaker. Petula was no help to him when it came to public relations. She was often considered too direct and descriptive in her speech. The art of negotiation with political rivals required skills of reasoning beyond either of their natural abilities. Neither Thaddeus nor Petula had good records when it came to putting people's minds at ease.

The previous summer proved to be a disastrous example of their lack of public relations skills. Mismanagement had depleted the revenue needed to fund the refurbishing of the ceiling in the central palace. Petula insisted that imposing a new tax on wheat exports was the only solution. Thaddeus reluctantly agreed and signed an executive order and delivered it to Simon, the Galilean sea region governor. In the ruling, Thaddeus indicated that any refusal to implement the export tax would be met with fierce reprisals.

The reaction by the merchants was immediate and hostile. With tariffs already low, merchants absorbed the costs of the extra tax levy. Their anger led to a chain reaction throughout the eastern seacoast. Exports decreased to marginal levels as traders moved on to cheaper partners along the Mediterranean.

As frustration increased, Thaddeus made attempts to address the concerns presented by merchants. When questioned, it became evident that Thaddeus knew very little about the trade market, which led to a lowering of public confidence. In the end, the emperor lowered the taxes in time to salvage local confidence. It was a reaction that Thaddeus did not see coming. Nor had anyone chosen to tell him.

"Summon Theo to take dictation," Thaddeus presently commanded his assistant, Theo, whom he now employed as a speechwriter following the tax debacle.

"Sir, you called," Theo said as he readily secured his place at the couch where Thaddeus and Petula were still reclining.

"Yes, I need dictation of a speech to be read at the town square." Thaddeus gestured for him to be seated at the end of the stone lounge.

"Whenever you are ready, I am ready," Theo responded with a quill pen already filled with ink and dripping nearby.

"Loyal subjects of Emperor Thaddeus," the dictation began.

Petula hesitantly kept her silence. *He has the worst opening statements,* she thought.

"This day, in the year of our Lord, Emperor Thaddeus, makes the following claim," said Thaddeus, as he reclined on the left side of the lounge as if doing so gave him more confidence in his words. Looking up at the ceiling, he continued, "As I complete my fifth year as your supreme leader, it is incumbent upon me to express my heartfelt gratitude for your loyal service to my administration."

He paused to collect his thoughts.

SAMUEL'S WOES

It took six days to disseminate the ordinance throughout the province. With its elaborate road system, Rome's regular use of foot carriers proved efficient enough for the message to reach most areas within a few days. Occasionally carriers used horses for more urgent matters. Word of mouth within the city complex also supplemented the official lines of communication. The announcement was met with mixed emotions among the crowd. Thaddeus, for the most part, was well-liked among the people. Compared to past rulers, there was not much to be concerned about with regard to his leadership. Some previous rulers had been much harsher with their brutal assaults on the citizens.

Samuel was standing in the square the day the messenger read the mandate. He wondered what was behind the words that on the surface seemed reassuring. *I wonder if this has something to do with Yeshua,* he thought.

The thought was too frightening to consider and thus he never spoke it into existence. Another part of him knew he must tell his son about the mandate. *Lately, Yeshua's performances have been benign and comical,* Samuel thought, *but the crowds have been growing and have summoned the attention of the emperor.*

His concerns were well-founded. The authorities frequently punished people for lesser infractions. The only question that remained in his mind had to do with whether Yeshua would listen to him or not.

"Something is going on," a bystander uttered as the messenger spoke. "The emperor never expresses his generosity using such public forums. What is this really about?"

Such social anxiety was common among the people; something internalized over generations. The general mantra among them was, "Peace before the war." Things have been much too quiet and peaceful over the last few years. War usually came in the form of losing some privileges or civil liberties. Such was the case during the insurgency caused by a group of Zealots.

The Zealots were a small militia of men from the countryside who often demonstrated in the streets at night under the cloak of darkness. Most of their actions caused minimal harm, usually mere distractions to the typical day-to-day routine. However, when one of the Zealots broke into the temple and started turning over the tax collectors' tables, swift reactions came from the Roman soldiers passing through the adjacent town.

Soldiers took only one of the Zealots into custody, but one was sufficiently effective. Fortunately, he avoided the routine public humiliation of crucifixion. Instead, his demise came mercifully quicker. In a field, just outside the east gate, his dismembered head rested peacefully on a wooden pole for all the other Zealots to see as they escaped to the countryside. The frozen expression on the dead Zealot's face showed that he died a painful and fearful death.

Chapter 4

The Name

AFTER SOME TIME, YESHUA abandoned his method of featuring multiple characters to develop a single personality as the central focus of each performance, often referred to as the hero. A lot of thought went into creating the character. Considering a name during the times required strategic and careful consideration of the social and historical implications. Whatever name he gave this character needed to be someone whom the audience could relate to across social and cultural boundaries.

Yeshua was keenly aware of Hellenistic forces' influence, although he did not know the formal term. However, he instinctively understood the impact the consequential blending of Judean and Roman culture was having on him and the region. He needed his character to be someone who represented the hopes and aspirations of the new hybridity seen in his people's lives. After reflecting for several days, a myriad of choices began to emerge. But the one name that seemed to most excite him was the simple Greek version of his name, Jesus.

Yes, Jesus! It was the perfect name for the character. Just the sound of it rolling from his lips sparked enthusiasm within Yeshua.

"I will call this character Jesus," he said.

To many, the obvious would be clear. However, since most people were illiterate and were not aware of the name's etymological significance, Yeshua was unsure of how to introduce this character. Jesus needed to be a Judean peasant, like the ordinary people, and a man who had a purpose that transcended culture and religion, bringing people together from different parts of the empire. The name carried many connotations among the native people. For most, it was a nonthreatening name that did not have a lot of political baggage. Unlike Moses, Maccabees, Herod, and other such names, Jesus was a common name with little historical significance. Like a blank canvas, Yeshua could shape and bend this character's trajectory in any form of his choosing.

YAEL OBJECTS

"Yason! You can't be serious!" exclaimed Yael. "How are you ever going to get people to take you seriously?" The look on Yael's face said it all. She was one of the most culturally sensitive group members, resisting the Roman-Greco culture's uncritical embrace. "We are always assimilating to these people. . .our food, our clothes, our bodies, our way of life."

Yael, young and idealistic about her Judean roots, cared less about the name's theatrical expediency.

"We need a character that appeals to a broader audience than the common peasantry that we have seen in the streets," Yeshua tried to explain. But Yael was persistently deviant.

"I don't like it at all. You are simply giving in to what is popular," she argued.

Disagreements between Yeshua and Yael were not uncommon. Yeshua expected such a reaction from her. But Yael thought it was more important to be heard than to have her way. She understood clearly that the decision was ultimately Yeshua's. Although more independent than most females her age, Yael believed in the traditional roles between men and women. She respected Yeshua, not only as a man but also his belief that something needed to change with regard to Roman oppression. In her mind, God chose Yeshua and gifted him with unique talents for acting and pretending. She admired his courage and willingness to take risks in critiquing the establishment. In the end, she trusted him without question. Jesus would be the name, and Yael accepted Yeshua's choice. At the time, she was unaware of what the cost of such loyalty would be.

"One more thing you should consider," Yael responded after pondering the idea. "Will this Jesus be called a messiah? Just wondering whether or not you had thought about it."

Yeshua had not given much thought about the messianic implications of the character named Jesus. He had given much thought about the Messiah his entire life, partially because of his name. He had lived in the shadow of what had become known to most people as only a myth. Yeshua had wondered why his father gave him the name.

"No, I have not given much thought to that. Why do you ask?" said Yeshua.

"People are going to start talking. Don't you think so?" Yael persisted. "They are always looking for some sign, wanting to believe it is true, and hoping it will be something that happens in their generation."

"I don't care what people think," Yeshua said forcefully.

He had not been active in the synagogue since his bar mitzvah. He never considered himself a religious person. So, he did not quite understand Yael's resistance.

Writing the first act with the new name proved to be an enormous task. First, Yeshua needed to decide whether this character would be a tragic hero or take on more comedic tones. Most of his performances used satire for entertainment purposes. Yeshua had cleverly learned the power of humor over the years. The task was always about getting people to laugh at themselves, something he was reluctant to abandon.

FROM MAN TO MYTH

It took Yeshua time to develop the character of Jesus as a young boy. But from all accounts, the Jesus character appeared to be growing in popularity. As the crowds grew, Yeshua delighted in the enthusiasm among the masses. The tension with Rome also increased. By now, soldiers regularly appeared at every street performance. Several of Yeshua's dramas had become so popular that repeat performances were required. For three years, Yeshua appeared in his performances so frequently that the boundaries between reality and theatre became fused in public perception. Even Yeshua himself often felt lost in his role as Jesus.

One such performance featured Jesus attending a wedding in a town called Cana.[1] Of course, any reference to Canaan invoked passions from Judeans, but its ending with Jesus turning water into wine was mostly met with amusement. Yeshua intentionally wanted to suggest a connection between the limited water supply in the villages and other social inequalities with the experience in Canaan.

Turning the water into wine had many political and social implications. Primarily, the miracle was performed after the mother's instructions, which in the eyes of the people, was a surprising display of subjugation to a woman's wishes. It proved to be both comical and offensive.

1. John 2:1–12.

The demand for Yeshua's performances began spreading beyond the streets and marketplace. Several aristocratic families living in the Roman province hosted evening parties featuring Yeshua's dramas. Because of their popularity, Yeshua could not always perform in them. Stand-in performers were often used, some trained by Yeshua, while others were freelancers. The most popular acts were performed at larger gatherings like festival celebrations, extending throughout the region. Each performance had a unique title, usually featuring the name Jesus as the main headline. Titles like, "The Boy Jesus," "Jesus: Prophet or King?," "The Sermon on the Mound," "Jesus: The Healing of the Man Born Blind," and "Jesus: Feeding the Five Thousand," were some of the biggest crowd-pleasers. Each performance shed some light on some area of injustice in the empire.

Yeshua could never have predicted the evolution of the character Jesus, although he intentionally fashioned him to be a symbol of oppression and a hybrid reflection of the growing influence of Greco-Roman culture on traditional Judaic values. Jesus, the man who befriended gentiles and outcasts, and placed their needs at the center of God's attention became the defining aspect of each act. Yeshua intentionally constructed his narratives to provoke the imagination of his audience and invited them to look at themselves and the world through a different lens.

Each drama's impact on the crowds was evidenced by the increasing calls for social reform among the people. No issue was off-limits in the dramas. The character Jesus had many complex dimensions and traits. He was a nontraditional Judean, poor, male, confrontational, compassionate, spiritual, earthy, and courageous. At the same time, Jesus had a dark side to his personality. He was persistently stubborn, demanding unreasonable sacrifices, egotistical, and was often narrow-minded in his perspective about the ancient laws. Yeshua realized that many of these traits mirrored his personality, as Alexia was so often willing to point out.

WOMEN AND DOGS

Yeshua gathered with his understudies to go over the next performance. It was the morning after Sabbath when most people remained indoors after the marketplace went silent. It was a time when Yeshua could retreat from the regular business of his father's pig farm and designing masonry walls. The anticipation of the next performances was especially intense among the understudies. Until now, the general acceptance among the people had been relatively good and the Roman authorities had been patient and tolerant. Yeshua kept the political rhetoric to a minimum without causing too much of a reaction from the soldiers and the loyalists who normally blended into the crowds.

"We must be careful how we introduce this next scene and its implications for people's lives," said Yeshua. "We have gained the approval of the people and the confidence of many in the empire." His voice conveyed a sense of calm and introspection. "Thank you all for your faithfulness so far."

As the sun began heating the Sabbath morning, Yeshua prepared them for the next performance. Yeshua was gaining confidence that his new character's popularity allowed him to expose the many facets of Judean oppression. It was the political implications of the man Jesus that fascinated him the most. Of course, in their culture, it was impossible to separate domestic life from political or religious life. Yet in his narratives, Yeshua was influenced by Hellenistic art and philosophy. He was neither fully aware nor conscious of the effect these had on the masses.

Yeshua was the product of a hybrid society and a generation of young actors who embraced past traditions but also submerged themselves in the new culture. Yeshua wanted his character to be a bridge-builder between the Judeans and other marginalized groups. Restoring peace in the land occupied by the Romans was the ultimate goal. So, Yeshua hoped that the character Jesus would give voice to the social yearnings of the poor while appealing to the attention of the socially affluent.

Thus far, his performances had garnered the attention of the people using satire and clandestine rhetoric. Some would say Yeshua played it too safe in that space between comfort and confrontation. Some of the lines and verses made people laugh and feel good to the extent that they did not catch the insult and critique that was embedded within the message. Most of the scenes were about the retelling of ancient stories called parables. Their messages were often cloaked in meanings that were only understandable to those who knew the life circumstances being portrayed.

For instance, the last drama was about a story of a woman confronting Jesus about his views of the poor.[2] Yeshua knew that to give women such a prominent voice in his acts bordered on theatric suicide, but he softened the blow by including a comedic exchange between Jesus and the woman.

"Even the dogs are given crumbs to eat beneath the tables of the wealthy," the woman said to Jesus as she berated him while walking down the street.

Yeshua added a dramatic effect by having her walk on all fours barking like a dog. The crowds laughed and were satisfied at the woman's imitation

---

2. Mark 7:24–30.

of the dog—she clearly posed no obvious threat to the status quo. They seemed blind to the critique she made about those in power.

Dialogue between the two lasted several minutes. Jesus, in the end, was persuaded by her protest and acknowledged the truth of her words. At the end of the scene, Jesus reached down to help the woman stand up. The crowd was silent as the poignant moment closed and the characters disappeared off the stage.

"That was wonderful," the soft reassuring voice came from behind Yeshua as he rushed off the stage. Its sound was paralyzing and yet familiar. He turned and there she stood, Alexia, the only person who could stop him in his tracks.

"Thank you," he replied. "I am glad you liked it."

"Yes, it was very interesting. Something new that I had not considered before. Women are dogs?" she smiled with one brow raised to indicate that the smile was not meant as approval but as a request for confirmation and clarification.

"Let us go for a walk to the seaport," Yeshua said. Alexia's escorts followed closely behind them.

As they walked, Yeshua explained the meaning of the scene. "No, that was not the point at all," he said.

As the change in Yeshua's disposition became more serious, Alexia regretted broaching the subject at a time when she had been enjoying his more playful demeanor.

"Dogs are used as a symbol of how the empire treats its citizens," explained Yeshua.

"Interesting way to show that," Alexia responded with interest and adoration of his analytical mind. "I assumed as much. But it is especially true for women and children." Alexia adjusted her posture to show a more serious intellectual side of herself.

"I agree. I wanted to show people how it felt to be on the bottom of the social ladder begging for bread, the very basic things we need for life." Yeshua explained.

"But I hope you know others are beginning to say things about your performances," Alexia said. She decided this was a good time to share with Yeshua the rumors coming from the governor's palace. "You need to be careful not to draw any more attention to yourself with such scenes."

Her words worried Yeshua. It was the first time Alexia had expressed any concerns or caution.

"Nothing to worry about. Most people are laughing too hard to notice what is being said. But for those who have ears to hear and eyes to see, I hope they get the message and spread it around to other enlightened people," Yeshua said with a bit of arrogance and pride.

"I don't want anything to happen to you or your family if word gets back to Thaddeus," Alexia persisted, voicing her concern.

"What does my family have to do with this? Is there something you are not telling me?" Yeshua was now frustrated with the idea that Alexia was not being completely honest with him.

"It is not that. I am telling you everything I know," Alexia insisted.

This was a half-truth. Alexia remembered the conversation last evening between her father and one of the members of the Sanhedrin. Rumors had leaked that Judean radicals were planning a revolt and that Yeshua's performances were simply a vehicle for transporting information from person to person without being noticed by the Roman authorities. Alexia was indeed unaware of the exact plans for dealing with the rumors, but she knew what the ramifications would be if there was even a perception that a revolt was being planned.

Alexia's warning and words were enough to give Yeshua pause, although he seldom took precautions. A strange paradox existed between them. On the one hand, he did not want her to worry about him, yet he loved her affection towards him. He intuitively knew that being in a dangerous position caused her to show him more affection. It was a delicate balance to maintain caution and concern.

JESUS MUST DIE

By now the character Jesus had become an apotheosis in the minds of many of his admirers. Some started comparing him with the ancient legends about the Messiah. Neither Yeshua, nor his disciples, anticipated such a rise in public popularity. However, Yeshua had been contemplating the evolution of the Jesus character. Then he made a stunning announcement to the other members of The Ekklesia.

"I have decided Jesus must die!" Yeshua said.

"Die!" Marco reacted, the youngest of the actors. "What do you mean die? How can you imagine such a thing?"

Marco expressed immediate and demonstrative frustration. He performed in many of the scenes that portrayed Jesus as a divine miracle worker who transformed the lives of the common people. In one of the acts, Marco portrayed a young man who was possessed by demons and lived among the tombs.[3] He met Jesus, who commanded the demons to come out of him. But the demons refused because they did not have another place to go.

Yeshua, wishing to poke fun at his father's business, had Jesus ordering the demons to leave the young man and possess the swine grazing on a nearby field. When the demons entered the swine, they became delirious and ran wild toward the sea where they all drowned. For Marco, this was his favorite role because it mirrored much of his personal life story. His admiration of the Jesus character made it more difficult to understand why Yeshua would have him die.

Yeshua tried to explain, "Jesus's appeal to the masses is becoming a threat to both the religious hierarchy and the Roman government. We know that Judeans did not practice any form of execution. However, the Romans conducted public executions of many of our heroes who fought and died for the liberation of the people. I ask you all: Who has kept us from our freedom?"

"The Romans, of course," Petras responded immediately.

"The Romans? Do you really believe that?" Yeshua gazed at each one of them. No one responded.

Yeshua then asked another probing question, "Who do people say Jesus is?"[4]

"Many people have come to see him as a prophet like Elijah," Yohanan answered. "Others said he reminded them of the Messiah."

"I have heard many compare him to Yohanan, the Baptist," Matthew spoke for the first time.

"This is good to know," Yeshua said to the group. "So then, my next question is this." He paused and stared intently at each of them. "Who do you say this Jesus is?"

"He is the hope of the people," Petras shouted. "You cannot take that away from the people!"

"Petras, you are as stubborn as a rock," Yeshua rebuked him but was careful not to raise his voice at the same level. He then laughed, "Jesus is only a character in a drama. How can he be the hope of the people? The people need something more than just a hopeful story."

Petras countered, "Yason, I know Jesus is only a character created by you. But your words have given us all something to live for and to fight for. They are not just stories, but thoughts and ideas to help people reimagine a different world for themselves." Petras continued to argue his point as if he was performing. "There is nothing to be gained through the death of Jesus."

3. Mark 5:1–20.
4. Matt 16:13–20.

"I agree with Petras," said James. "Jesus has become real in the eyes of many. His words have touched lives and changed hearts. He has brought us together as a new unified community."

Yeshua paused before responding. He bent down on one knee and drew images in the sand. The others gathered around him to see what was happening. Yeshua never learned to read or write. However, he was a gifted artist and designer. He possessed an incredible ability to use words and metaphors to create pictures in the minds of his audiences.

"Tell me what you see?" Yeshua asked.

The group crowded around him to look more intentionally at the drawings on the ground. Petras recognized the image first, "It is an image of a fish."

"Yes, that's what I see," says Yohanan.

Yeshua looked surprised. "Yes, you are right. It is a fish."

"So, what are you saying?" James asked.

"Yes, Yason, what does this mean?" Petras joined in.

"What do the prophets say? Give a man a fish and you feed his family for a day," said Yeshua.

"But teach him to fish," Yael began, "and he will feed the entire village for a lifetime."

"Exactly!" Yeshua explained. "I never anticipated the character Jesus would become embraced by so many people. I did not think so many would come to see him as the messianic figure of the past. The people have turned Jesus into a god. They think he can save them. But he cannot! He is just a man! But he can inspire them to save themselves."

Everyone silently looked down at the ground as Yeshua continued to explain why Jesus must die in the next performance. "His martyrdom will serve as an example of the suffering our people have endured. His death will be a vivid reminder of the injustices that we live under every day."

"Yes, but we've had martyrs before. They come and they go, and they are forgotten," Yohanan uttered.

"True, but the death of Jesus will be different. He will die under circumstances that will provoke the passions of the people. You see, it is not the Romans alone who oppress our people. But it is the collusion between the Romans and our own leaders that reinforces our disenfranchisement," Yeshua explained.

All of this was beginning to sound dangerously close to getting them all arrested. Most of the men were intrigued by the risk. But one of them, Thomas, had serious doubts. Provoking the Roman government was often suicidal, and Thomas had no intention of putting himself at risk.

Until then, he sat quietly under a tree behind the circles of the others who stood and sat in various positions around Yeshua as he spoke to them. Thomas quietly tootled on his flute, barely audible above the discussion among them, but loud enough to distract him from the conversation. Finally, he broke his silence.

Standing and facing Yeshua, Thomas said, "Yason, I mean you no disrespect. We have all followed your training and guidance. We have all benefited from the popularity of the man named Jesus. But what you are asking us now causes me to question your motives," Thomas walked closer to Yeshua.

Yeshua did not wait for the closing proximity between them to occur, "What do you mean my motives, Thomas? I believe it has always been clear to everyone why I do what I do. None of you have ever questioned my motives until now."

Thomas quickly responded, "I do not doubt that you are sincere in wanting to stir the hopes of the people. You have done that very thing. None of us would have ever thought to portray a messianic figure who can speak to the hearts of both gentiles and Judeans. Never did I anticipate that he would bring together such different nationalities of people. I believe all of this to be good and true. But Yeshua, I wonder now whether or not you are doing this for selfish reasons alone."

Yeshua exclaimed, "Selfish! In what way am I being selfish?"

Thomas continued and did not defer to the group, "I think you are only doing this to bring attention to yourself. The death of Jesus will only bring glory to Yason!"

Then Petras joined the argument, wishing to diffuse the tension between the two men, "Yason, Thomas doesn't mean selfish." He spoke while pointing his finger, "Thomas, you know that is not true." He then turned to Yeshua. "I think what he wants to say is we are concerned about your well-being and the impact this could have on your future as an actor."

Thomas looked at Petras and Yeshua, but he refused to say more. He wondered if he had already said too much. So, instead of persistently arguing his position, he retreated to the tree that comforted him up until now and sat back down, looking away from them.

He finally said, "Maybe selfish was too strong of a word. But I cannot see how any good can come of this. I don't understand why Jesus must die. Who will benefit?"

Yeshua delighted at the question raised by Thomas and seized the opportunity to make his case. "I cannot fully explain to you all exactly why Jesus must die and why we must do this together. All I ask of you is to trust me."

Chapter 5

The Tradition

AFTER THE MEETING, MATTHEW, Thomas, and Petras continued discussing the character named Jesus. They all lived north of the village and often accompanied each other on the trip to the city.

"I don't like this new direction Yeshua is taking in his performances," Matthew said to Petras as they strolled toward the North gate.

"I agree with you. It doesn't make sense to me, but we should trust him. He has never been wrong about developing a character," Petras said.

"Can we truly trust him? What if he is wrong? What if he is not the man we think he is?" Thomas asked.

"What do you mean?" Petras inquired. "Look at all that he has taught us about acting and presenting ourselves to the public."

Matthew remained skeptical despite Petras's defense of Yeshua. "He does not follow the traditions. I know he is Judean like all of us, but his ways of thinking are like the gentiles. His dramas are often about being good to the sinners and to those who are not like you."

"What you have said is true," professed Petras. "But this is a new day. Sometimes things must change to allow for the new ways of the world. Even the old teachings said to be welcoming to the foreigner and immigrants among you."

"I know, but it did not mean to become them. This Jesus is too much like a gentile. His character even uses many of the popular expressions. Only a Greek tragedy would allow the main character to suffer and die," Matthew continued. "It is not our way!"

Petras decided to express aloud what he had been contemplating since earlier in the day. "Matthew, you have to look to the future and not the past. Besides, the past is not as good as we often think it was. Our people have suffered much in the past, mostly because of our own choices. Four hundred years of slavery in Egypt and wandering in the wilderness did not teach us anything. Captivity in Babylonia and the Persian exile were not good years for us. The Torah teaches that there were only six good days, and God rested on the seventh. Those are the only good-ole days in our tradition. I welcome the fresh new perspective that Yeshua has given to us. I am glad he trusts us enough to let us perform in his dramas. You should feel the same way."

"Perhaps you are right," Matthew said as they continued to move through the North gate. "I have often thought that this Jesus character needed to honor the traditions of our people. Most of our people have lived long enough to know the ancient stories about Moses, Elijah, and Isaiah the prophet. They were all mighty men who performed miraculous works of God. This Jesus has not performed a single great miracle. Some demonstration of prophetic power would make the character much more convincing."

"You should talk with Yeshua about this," Petras responded. "He cares more about words and their meaning. The long speeches are boring at times, so miracles would help make Jesus more exciting."

"I agree with Matthew," said Thomas. "The Romans understand only one thing, power. If Yeshua wants to get the emperor's attention, he will need to give this Jesus some power. He needs to heal some people, cast out a few demons, or raise a man from the dead."

Petras listened and nodded to signal his agreement. After listening for a while, he interjected, "Matthew, you are a well-respected and educated scholar. Go to Yason and explain this to him. Offer to write some of the scenes to show him that what you say is true."

"He won't listen to me. He likes doing things his way."

"What harm can there be?" Petras argued. "Even if he does not listen to you, at least you can sleep at night knowing that you tried. Who knows? Years from now, you may be writing narratives of your own with lots of signs and wonders."

"You are right. I will do this," Matthew said begrudgingly.

The three finally reached the northern village and separated at the fork in the road. Petras continued to think about the conversation with Matthew. He now had doubts about Matthew's commitment and loyalty to the ways of Jesus. It is hard for some to let go of the traditions. Petras decided to keep his eye on Matthew and Thomas. Perhaps he would share about their conversation with Yeshua.

JOSEPHUS

Yeshua clearly understood that his followers did not have a common understanding of who Jesus was in the performances, although they had all performed the role at various times. He could not expect them to fully understand the impact that the death of Jesus would have on the masses, revealing the truth about their circumstances.

Several of his scenes had hinted at the corruption among many Judean leaders. For instance, in one drama, Jesus spoke with a Judean leader around the subject of personal transformation. He belonged to a sect of pious Judeans called the Pharisees. Most people highly regarded the Pharisees, who believed in strict adherence to the ancient laws. Even without Yeshua naming the Pharisee character, everyone knew the scene was about Nicodemus, who was the personification of the traditional Judean beliefs.[1] The encounter with Jesus showed the need for change from the old way of thinking.

The scene unfolded at night to represent Nicodemus's inability to see and perceive new ideas. Yeshua wanted people to know that holding onto old and irrelevant ideas only left people blinded to their current oppression. He also intentionally showed how a highly regarded religious leader came to Jesus for insight and answers. Instead, Jesus said to the Pharisee, "You must be born again to see what God is doing among you." The Pharisee was baffled by the concept of being born again and deferred to the wisdom of Jesus.

The Pharisees were furious with Yeshua when they heard about the performances. Flavius Josephus, one of the leaders of the Pharisees, was concerned about the impact Yeshua's dramas were having on civic relations with the Romans. His efforts at diplomacy were legendary. Things had been quiet for the last few years since Thaddeus tolerated many of their customs and holy festivals.

Josephus decided to visit Samuel with the hope that he could persuade Yeshua to abandon his public performances. The popularity of the new character Jesus troubled Josephus. It took a day's journey to travel by foot to Samuel's farm from Yerushalayim's westside, where Josephus taught ancient history at the local synagogue. Few people traveled to the out country where Samuel raised his pigs. Not only did the smell deter many from the trip, but the moral implications of a Judean raising swine was difficult for most orthodox people to tolerate. Josephus felt compelled to make this visit to see Samuel. Too much was at stake.

---

1. John 3:1–21.

Once he was in sight of the farm, Josephus pushed ahead up the gravel path toward the gate leading to the house. Fortunately, Samuel's home was positioned near the front of the entrance so that one could reasonably visit his home without much exposure to the stench and filthy conditions. These were unavoidable once going a few lengths beyond the main house.

"Greetings. You must be Samuel," Josephus said in polite address. Samuel had already seen him coming up the path, and decided to meet him at the gate.

"Yes, I am him."

"My name is Josephus."

"I know who you are," Samuel interrupted. "Everyone knows who you are. So, what do I owe the honor of your presence at my doorstep? A well-respected man like yourself would not dare show his face around the property of a despised swine owner unless there was a serious matter at hand."

"I have a matter of great importance to discuss with you. I have traveled far to speak with you face-to-face about this. May I enter your home?"

Josephus was aware of the possible consequences to his reputation if someone were to recognize him standing outside the home of a pig farmer. He hoped to have a conversation with Samuel inside his house out of view of the neighbors.

"Yes, of course." Samuel finally gave consent and gestured for Josephus to follow him into the home where they sat down on the floor. "Miriam, we have a visitor," Samuel yelled to his wife in the adjacent room. The sound of his voice caused a slight quiver to run through her body.

"Yes, Samuel, I will bring some bread and wine for you and your guest," said Miriam.

Miriam pretended not to know who the stranger was that was visiting their home. She did not need to know. It was none of her business to know. She automatically responded in the acceptable way wives did when their husbands entertained guests. At least, this was what she wanted her husband to think.

Contrary to customs, Miriam knew exactly who the man in the other room was, and more than Samuel, she knew why he visited their home. It was about Yeshua and his performances. But Miriam kept this information to herself. She did not want to disrespect her husband in front of a guest by revealing she knew something that he did not know. So, she silently obeyed the traditions.

Josephus spoke first. "Thank you for your hospitality and for letting me enter your home. I have traveled many miles to talk with you about your son." His expressions of alacrity surprised Samuel.

"Oh, really? What about my son is interesting enough for you to travel so far?" Samuel responded.

"Your son is quite talented. I have observed a couple of his stories and found them to be very thought-provoking." Josephus said. His words were surprising to Samuel, but also calculated. "The first one was the most impressionable. It involved the main character, Jesus, and his encounter with a man named Zacchaeus, a tax collector.[2] The performance took place in the center of the market where an old sycamore tree stood for many years. The actor in Zacchaeus's role, I think his name is Matthew, climbed up on the branch of the sycamore tree because he was so short. When Jesus looked up at the man, recognizing who he was, he invited himself to his house for dinner."

"So, what did you think of the story?" Samuel carefully inquired.

"I was impressed with the staging and the symbolism. As you know, tax collectors are not well-liked among us and cannot be trusted because of their allegiance to Roman rule. The Jesus character is growing in popularity. His message is divisive and sets a bad example. There were almost two hundred citizens gathered around the square that day. I wondered how they accepted the idea of Jesus volunteering to have dinner in the home of such a despised person."

Josephus paused as if he expected a reaction from Samuel and wondered what he thought about the tax collectors as a businessman. As they talked, Miriam entered the room, addressed her husband first, and then waited for Samuel to introduce her to Josephus.

"Samuel, I have your wine and bread for you and your guest," she said. This was Samuel's cue.

"Thank you, Miriam. This is Josephus. He has come to visit me and talk about Yeshua's performances." Samuel kept his introductions short and straightforward.

"It was so nice of you to come to visit with us today and share with us about our son. He is a very talented performer," Miriam said with an expression of pride on her face. "Ever since he was a young boy Yeshua loved reciting the ineffable words of the prophets and the Psalms. He not only knew the words but could perform the characters of the stories. My favorite has always been—"

Miriam wanted to continue, but Samuel interrupted her. "Miriam, Josephus is a busy man and does not have long to visit. Some other time. Thank you." Samuel was polite but dismissive. He turned his attention back to Josephus. "And you were saying?"

2. Luke 19:1–10.

Josephus, trying to recover his attention from the story Miriam was about to tell him, continued with his reflections about Yeshua's performances.

"The performance was impressive, thought-provoking, and dangerous," he said.

"Dangerous?" Samuel immediately responded.

"Yes, dangerous. That is why I came here today. I wanted to talk with you about his activities and the possibility that they might incite subversion among some of the more radical of our people," said Josephus.

"Who might be these radicals?"

"You know. For instance, the Zealots. Their founder, Judah of Gaulanitis, has inspired many such groups who wish to use violence to incite reform. Your son's actions could cause some of this same behavior among the people. So, you must talk to him and get him to change or stop all of his performances before something bad happens."

"And what bad thing might happen?" Samuel asked.

"You know what I am talking about," Josephus said in a raised voice. "You have seen for yourself what the Roman government does whenever it perceives anything to be a threat to its power. As his father, you should be especially concerned."

"What does that mean?"

Josephus, an astute diplomat, was careful in how he chose words to convey his real concern. Although he had no personal interest in Yeshua's performances or Samuel, Josephus wanted to make sure that his words impacted Samuel enough to get his attention.

"You know for yourself that if the government determined Yeshua to be a threat to them, they would not hesitate to arrest him, or worse, take his life," Josephus warned.

"Yes, I am aware of that. What does that have to do with me?" Samuel responded.

Josephus put the wine goblet down on the ground between Samuel and himself. He leaned forward to speak within ear range, and he said, "Well, you are a rich man. Your success depends on Roman generosity. Your meat is sold in many markets, both inside and outside the cities. Let's be honest. You would not have been as successful if it had not been for the Roman authorities' permission. What do you think will happen to your business and your wealth if your son is arrested? Do you think the gentiles will continue to buy your meat? Do you think anyone will have anything to do with you? The Judeans already hate you. The Romans only use you for their selfish means. Have you not considered these things?"

Samuel thought quietly for a moment about what Josephus said to him. He had not given much thought about the personal and business repercussions of Yeshua's actions. He felt torn between wanting to defend his son and facing the reality of the situation. Samuel sat on the floor as he allowed the words to run their course through his mind and down to his stomach.

Josephus is right. This could not only hurt my business but bring danger to all Judeans, Samuel thought.

As the words began to sink and settle in his stomach, the rumbling noises became audible. He needed to relieve himself of the anxiety. Fortunately, Josephus also sensed the need to end their conversation and stood up to signal an end to his visit.

"Think about these things. I know that you will do the right thing," Josephus reassured himself as he prepared to leave.

Miriam was still in the corner of the room. She wanted to speak up and defend her son, but she did not want to disgrace her husband. She felt sorry for him as he sat with a look of despair on his face. She intuitively knew what he was feeling, but there was nothing she could do to save him from the truth.

After Josephus left, Samuel stood up. His stomach was cramping and begging for some relief. The sounds in his stomach seeped out of him and filled the room with an odor even the swine could not tolerate. But as a pig farmer, by comparison, the smell went unnoticed.

"I will talk to him," Miriam finally broke her silence.

"No, I am his father. I will do it."

"But I am his mother. He will listen to me. If you talk to him, he will only argue with you." Miriam pleaded with Samuel and placed her hand on his stomach to soothe his pain. It felt good to him.

"No, I will talk to him," Samuel insisted.

SAMUEL'S WAIT

Samuel concluded that he must talk with his son that evening and share his conversation with him. Out of mutual respect, Yeshua would give him an audience but likely would not consider changing the dialogues. His determination to awaken pride and hope within the people underlay each stanza in his stories. Samuel pondered whether consulting with Miriam before talking to Yeshua might be the wiser course of action.

Meanwhile, at the farm, Samuel waited anxiously for Yeshua to return for the day to talk with him and persuade him to stop his antagonistic performances. He rehearsed the logic of his appeal to Yeshua, who usually listened better to reasoned arguments than he did to passionate pleas to respect their traditions. Samuel stayed prepared to assert his parental right to protest any actions by his children regardless of whether they agreed with him.

I wish things were like the old days, Samuel thought, *when sons obeyed the wishes of their fathers without questioning or challenging them. I will not tolerate any of his actions that reflect badly on this household.* His mind continued to race through all the possible arguments and justifications. *I must not allow the safety and security of our village to be jeopardized by the reckless behavior of one member.*

The conclusion of his logic pointed in only one direction. It was too painful for Samuel even to consider. He feared more than anything what he would have to do if Yeshua refused to listen to his line of reasoning.

"I will have no other choice than to ask him to leave," he said to himself, allowing the words to escape his mind and whisper upon his lips. The very possibility of asking his son to leave home caused a nervous shiver to reverberate through his core.

Suddenly Samuel heard the distant sound of someone walking outside. It was evening now, and the sun was fully set. The wind picked up slightly, resulting in the clanging sounds of soft metal objects draped along most villager's houses. Samuel knew it was Yeshua coming home. It was time to confront his son. The wind seemed to increase the closer Yeshua came to the home of his father. Samuel quickly said a short prayer for affirmation from God that he was making the right decision. In his mind, all the prophets of old and new were on his side.

As Samuel waited in anticipation for Yeshua's arrival and the dread of having to confront him, the sound of the distant footsteps changed tone suddenly. The soft sandy walkway leading to their house was infiltrated with tiny rocks. Therefore, each step sounded a faint crunch that got louder as the person approached the front entrance.

Over the years, Samuel had developed a heightened sense of awareness of the sound of footsteps. He had learned to hear who was coming and how far away they were. Yeshua had a distinct walking pattern and stepped at a different pace than Miriam, who had a much softer and slower stride. Both of their personalities were detected in the sound of their walking. Samuel never gave much thought to this skill of detection until now, when suddenly the impressions outside changed and multiplied. Instead of one person, there was the sound of many feet on the gravel and sand.

Who is coming home with Yeshua? He never mentioned anyone would be joining us for the evening meal, Samuel thought.

Silently Samuel pondered the noise for a few moments before rushing to the entrance to look outside. As he moved to the door to see who was with Yeshua, he was slightly annoyed that whoever was with him would dare interrupt the anticipated conversation. Instead of rushing out the front door, Samuel decided to peer out the window adjacent to the door, as was often his manner.

Looking out the window, to his surprise, were several Roman soldiers gathering around Yeshua. They were at the opening of the front gate, making it impossible for Samuel to hear the conversation. His first instinct was to yell and question their presence immediately. But he also knew the risk if such actions were misunderstood as interference in the empire's affairs. Part of him felt helpless while another part was relieved that finally the soldiers would settle the matter.

The harsh reprimand of the soldiers would supersede the stressful conversation with his son. They would likely only warn him about his performances, reiterating what he had been trying to tell Yeshua all along. Samuel delighted in the possibility of convincing Yeshua that his pursuit of acting was too risky and dangerous and forcing him to reconsider his actions. Then it happened.

One of the soldiers began yelling at Yeshua, "How dare you mock the authority of the emperor."

Yeshua returned the rebuke, "That's outrageous. I am simply a street performer providing much-needed entertainment for people in the market. I have no idea what you are talking about." Yeshua raised his voice to emphasize his defiance.

Thinking the argument would escalate out of control, the soldier quickly struck Yeshua on his right cheek with the back of his left hand. The sting penetrated through his jawbone, causing vibration up to his brain. Yeshua fell to the ground in pain. Samuel stood frozen in the doorway, paralyzed by the mere shock of seeing his son fall helplessly to the ground.

Several emotions surged through Samuel as he watched Yeshua lay motionless on the ground. Fear and anger were the most prevalent of the feelings—fear of what could happen to Yeshua, and anger at him for provoking the authorities.

Slowly, as Yeshua returned to consciousness, he struggled to stand erect and steady himself before the same soldier who had just emasculated him, Yeshua did something no one expected. He stood before the soldier and made direct eye contact with him. The silence was the only entity that stood between them.

Yeshua showed no emotion on his face, something he learned to do from years of performing. His blank stare stirred something within the soldier that immediately disarmed and confused him. Knowing how disrespectful it was to look a soldier in the eye, Yeshua turned his head to offer his left cheek for the next blow. This subtle act of bold deviance seemed more baffling to the soldier than anything else. Yeshua held his pose for what appeared to be minutes before turning his head. He remained silent as everyone waited for the next move.

Samuel was astonished at his son's command of the situation. It was the first time he realized that the boy had come of age. He was a man now, not a reckless young boy. He remained paralyzed by the moment. He waited to see what the next step would be. Would the soldiers decide that Yeshua posed no real threat and leave, or would Samuel need to intervene?

The lead soldier must save face and command of the legion. He had orders to bring Yeshua in for questioning and broke the silence. "Arrest him," he announced with a loud shout, reclaiming his authority over the situation. The other soldiers moved quickly in response to his command. One grabbed Yeshua by the arm and another stood at his back to make sure he had nowhere to run.

At this point, Samuel made his move to the outside of the house to ask what charges were against Yeshua. Before he could say a word, Yeshua's eyes fixed on his and the unspoken message was clear, "Don't say a word. I can handle this. I am a man now."

The movements of the soldiers to restrain Yeshua were swift and or-chestrated. The arrest seemed strategically choreographed as if rehearsed. Yeshua offered no resistance, which added to the predetermined effect. The magistrate's office was about ten miles away on foot. It would be closed at this time of the evening, so any proceedings would have to wait until the next day. For now, the matter would be handled locally, and a report filed with Simon the governor the following day. It would be left up to the governor to decide whether to press charges or report the case to the emperor.

Chapter 6

Empire

THE LONG DARK TRAIL to the magistrate's quarters took most of the night to walk. Yeshua walked in silence, never offering any resistance to the wishes of the soldiers. Once the group arrived, they led Yeshua to a small building north of the magistrate's office. More satisfactory than expected, the room was comfortable with a soft bed on the wooden floor.

The jail cell was a welcome relief from the long walk in sweat-filled garments, with its cool concrete floors and breezy hallways. The stark contrast between the elite and the peasantry was evident by the modest accommodations.

When morning broke, Yeshua felt rested after having enjoyed the basic comforts of Roman living. He ate fresh fish and bread for breakfast, better than most people had in the village. He had received formal and polite treatment thus far. Part of this enraged Yeshua and made him more determined to speak about the disparities through his narratives. Around the eleventh hour, the magistrate arrived and summoned Yeshua to make his appearance.

The guards came and opened Yeshua's cell. The lock, surprisingly, was barely secured, to the point that Yeshua regretted not attempting an escape, although it would have served no real purpose. The short passageway inside the jail led to a backdoor exit. The morning sun shining through the corridor temporarily blinded Yeshua as he emerged from the darkness of the jail. It reminded him of the blindness experienced by his people every day under Roman oppression.

Lately, the mornings were hotter than most days, a sure sign of the changing season. Sweat poured down Yeshua's face and ran into his eyes. He quickly raised his hands to wipe the sweat from his brow before it stung his eyes. Yeshua was surprised to note that his hands were no longer bound as they had been during the journey across the desert on the previous evening. Although this was Yeshua's first time in custody, nothing was what he had expected. He did not experience the expected inhumane treatment and strict military-like decorum.

Soon the soldiers marched Yeshua expeditiously across the courtyard, one on each side and another to his rear. They entered the magistrate's office's main chamber, as the apparent change in the sound of their footsteps on the pavement signaled that they were now entering another level of Roman luxury.

Before reaching the magistrate's office, Yeshua was ordered to sit down on the floor of the corridor. He offered no resistance. Each step seemed well organized and ritualized, and the pageantry of the moment impressed Yeshua. Instead of feeling like a prisoner, Yeshua felt more like an actor performing an expected role. He had come to realize that much of life in Palestine was about acting one's part in a drama. The Roman authorities served their role as oppressors while the citizenry was complicit in their submission.

"Where is the prisoner?"

The magistrate's voice echoed throughout the chamber. Yeshua was still sitting on the floor in the corridor and nearly falling asleep. The sound of the magistrate's voice awakened him and signaled that Roman jurisprudence was in action.

"Sir, he is present and ready to be questioned," one of the guards standing in the doorway leading to a square room responded without hesitancy, standing at the appropriate position of respect.

"Bring him in," he ordered one of his subordinates, who in turn motioned for Yeshua to stand and move toward the entrance of the magistrate's chamber.

The soldiers stood on both sides of Yeshua as he proceeded toward the magistrate. Rome appointed magistrates throughout the province as the gatekeepers of the judicial process. They heard cases and domestic situations that were considered harmless threats to the emperor's power. Often, they were advice-givers, marriage counselors, or mediators in land disputes.

It appeared that Yeshua's activities had not reached the same level of seriousness or concern from the Roman authorities. Therefore, the magistrate was only responsible for collecting information about the person suspected of rebellious actions against the emperor. Fortunately for Yeshua, the magistrate had little power over his personhood. Unfortunately for Yeshua, this magistrate wanted Yeshua to think he had more power than he actually possessed.

"State your name and your father's surname," ordered the magistrate. There was a slight pause before Yeshua gave a response.

"My name is Yason, son of Samuel of Nazareth." His voice was calm and even-toned.

"Nazareth?" the magistrate asked. Then he chuckled, "Can any good thing come from there?" The other guards smiled slightly before returning to their official facial expression.

At first, the magistrate did not show much awareness of Yeshua's presence. He did not make any gesture to signal approval or dismissiveness because Yeshua came from one of the remote villages in the region. He continued without much regard for the proceedings while never looking directly at Yeshua.

"You have been summoned here today because of instigating disruptive activities in the marketplace during the normal hours of business," explained the magistrate. "You are appearing before me this day to determine the level of seriousness of your activities. This is not a formal hearing of any criminal charges. Therefore, you are not afforded any legal representation or defense. As an officer of the emperor and magistrate charged by Simon's office, the governor, I am sworn by the court to explain to you the situation that brought you here today and make sure you know the full ramifications of any legal violations. Do you understand?"

Yeshua fully understood the proceedings. He felt no intimidation by a local court official. "I understand," he said.

"Can you read or write your name?" Literacy was a measure of social status. So this became a standard question to ask before interrogating a person to assess whether or not the individual posed any real threat. Knowing this, Yeshua responded, "No, I cannot."

This was not entirely true, but Yeshua assumed the magistrate knew that most people in his village did not read or write. They maintained an oral culture in which verbal communication and memory were the preferred means of conveying information, which caused them to appear less threatening to the dominant culutre. Asking such a question about reading and writing could be a means of entrapment, something Yeshua wanted to avoid. Yeshua read some Greek but mostly spoke in Aramaic. Greek was the preferred language of the marketplace. As a child, he observed his father's savvy negotiating skills among the market's diverse clientele. He knew the more straightforward answer would be to say no.

"Do you need an interpreter? Can you understand everything I am saying to you?" the magistrate asked, pressing the issue.

"I can understand everything you are saying to me, Sir," Yeshua answered respectfully as to make this process as easy for the magistrate as for himself.

"Alright. We will proceed," the magistrate said, letting out a big sigh. Yeshua's discovery of his ploy to entrap him frustrated him. "Yeshua, son of Samuel, has been accused of provoking dissension among the people through your so-called 'street theatre.' Is this true?" He asked.

Yeshua paused before responding. "Yes, it is true that I am a street performer. I have been for several years now. But no, I have no intention of provoking any dissension among my audience. My purpose and aim are to entertain my audience and to make them happy." Yeshua's response was wise and calculated not entirely to deny the charges, but to reframe his answers in disarming ways.

"So, you deny the accusations made against you?" The magistrate forcefully asked. "Do you understand the ramifications of bearing false witness in my court?" The magistrate's voice was calm, but he chose words so as to intimidate Yeshua and establish his authority over him.

"Yes, I understand fully. And I stand by my answer," Yeshua answered.

Yeshua never blinked or bowed. He was no doubt indefatigable in declaring his innocence and refused to play into the magistrate's hands.

After several minutes of silence, the magistrate finally spoke. "You will be given a warning for now. However, rest assured that we will be watching you and monitoring your actions. If any word comes back to me that you are engaging in any radicalized activity against the kingdom, then you will be subdued immediately."

The words of the magistrate seemed not to pierce the guarded expression on Yeshua's face. Yet, it was a relief for Yeshua to know that he would not spend another evening in the oppressors' royal accommodations.

"Release this man," the magistrate ordered.

The soldiers moved expeditiously to escort Yeshua out of the presence of the magistrate. As they moved into the inner courtyard, one of the soldiers whispered lowly a warning of his own in Yeshua's ear.

"Consider yourself fortunate this time, peasant," he said.

It was not clear to Yeshua what the soldier was talking about. Roman use of euphemisms was always confusing to most Judeans. Yeshua dared not ask anything that could potentially prolong the process of his dismissal. Word of his arrest and interrogation ordinarily would have ended at the office of the local magistrate. However, with close ties to the emperor, a sinister opportunistic personality had been waiting for such a situation as Yeshua's to exploit for personal gain and power.

ALEXIA'S ANGST

As she sat on the floor of her bedroom at her father's palace, Alexia worried about Yeshua's fate. She knew about his interrogation at the magistrate's office. Her father heard about the plans to arrest him for questioning. Alexia remained silent about their relationship. Her father must never know about her love for Yeshua. She loved her father and would not do anything to dishonor him.

Alexia also resented the way he colluded with the Roman empire. Her life had been one of luxury. It was all because of her father's political savvy. For this, she had always been grateful. She despised the way her father used the people as a ploy to gain power and influence with the emperor. Her father knew nothing about her feelings toward him. Like her mother, she learned to stay in her place and enjoy the comforts of being the daughter of a Roman citizen.

It was getting close to evening and there was still no word from Yeshua. It had been weeks since his detention. So Alexia decided to go for a walk with her guardian escorts toward the marketplace. She knew the pathway that led to the place where Yeshua usually practiced his lines, far removed from the market exchange's noise. Large cedar trees on each side fortified the path leading to the clearing. Walking down the path gave a false sense of security as the tree branches blanketed the view of the sky. Knowing it would soon be too late, Alexia ordered her escorts to buy fresh produce at the market before the merchants closed for the day. She quickly made her way down the darkened path, hoping to find Yeshua.

As the sky darkened, making it unsafe to travel alone, the large cedar trees concealed any potential dangers that could be lurking in its foliage. Alexia walked faster as she approached the opening of the wall of trees. The sounds of the market began to fade in the background and the silence of the countryside engulfed the evening air. On the other side of the passage through the cedar trees was a large mound overlooking the next town. When standing on the mound one's voice echoed throughout the valley, but not far enough to be heard by anyone.

Just as Alexia suspected, Yeshua was there on the mound practicing his lines for his next performance. Since he was a man of routines, it was easy to predict his whereabouts, a trait that made Yeshua both dependable and vulnerable.

He bellowed each line,

Blessed are you when you are reviled,
and all manner of evil is done against you.
Blessed are the peacemakers,
for they shall be called the children of God.
Blessed are the meek, for you shall inherit the earth!

Alexia raised her voice loudly in unison as she approached Yeshua, "Blessed are those who tell their women where they are and let them know they are safe."

Alexia's sudden interruption startled Yeshua, but he immediately recognized her voice and embraced her.

"Truly, you are blessed with my love," Yeshua said.

He smiled as he turned around and rushed toward Alexia, who was now standing at the base of the mound. They embraced and kissed for what seemed like an eternity, excited and relieved to see one another. It was not until Yeshua saw her that he remembered how much he longed for her. He was overwhelmed with emotions that he had attempted to suppress by directing his attention to preparing for upcoming performances.

"Where are your escorts?" Yeshua inquired.

"I was so worried about you, so I sent them to the market while I came to see if you were here," Alexia, gasping for air while Yeshua's lips pressed firmly against her lips. "I heard all about your visit to the magistrate."

"What did you hear?" Yeshua inquired.

"That you said nothing to defend yourself. It made you look guilty," Alexia said, still frustrated with Yeshua for his silence and absence.

"I am guilty. But I knew the magistrate's intentions," Yeshua said with a confident smirk on his face. "I knew he was trying to trap me with his questions. I know my rights, and I know how much the magistrate wants to keep his job. What is your father saying?"

"He is not saying much," Alexia answered. "He just thinks you are harmless, and your performances are meaningless. He understands why you do what you do, but he does not want Thaddeus to come down on him. My father is not a very religious man. He cares more about politics than he does God or the people who worship God."

Alexia's voice seemed to relax for the moment. She felt torn between her respect for her father's position and her love for Yeshua.

"Why have I not heard from you? Are you angry with me?" Alexia asked Yeshua.

"No, of course not. I am not angry with you," Yeshua replied. "But I am afraid of what could happen to you if the accusations become more serious.

When I left Galilee after being questioned by the magistrate, I realized that I needed to be more careful about my actions. I don't want to think about what would happen if your father found out about us." Yeshua turned his back to Alexia to demonstrate how painful the thought of life without her would be for him.

"Nothing will happen to me. I am his daughter and his favorite. Although disappointed and angry, I know my father. He will not take out his anger on me," she said to reassure Yeshua.

Alexia had repositioned herself directly in front of Yeshua's face. She refused to allow him not to look her in the eyes. Yeshua maneuvered away from Alexia's stare.

"I know that. He will take his anger out on me! And you will never see me again. Nor will anyone ever see me again," said Yeshua.

"Don't you think I know that?" Alexia rebuffed. "Don't you know that I love you more than I fear my father? I will never allow anything to happen to you or us. If he finds out about us, then we will just run away together." Yeshua was surprised to hear Alexia speak so confidently. For the past few weeks, Alexia had thought much about what would happen if her father discovered the truth.

"Where will we go?" Yeshua argued.

"Far away from the reaches of the empire. I know people who will help us." Alexia tried to convince Yeshua. "Just don't leave me again without saying something and letting me know what is going on."

"You are an amazing and stubborn woman," said Yeshua.

He turned to face Alexia head-on then pressed himself against her body. He resumed kissing and sucking on her lips and mouth as if a desperate animal in need of food. Alexia was startled not only by his passionate kisses but the bulge behind his robe that was now penetrating the slit between her thighs. She felt the inspissation of his loins as they both fell to the ground in each other's embrace. They made love on the side of the hill.

Blessed are the pure in heart, for they shall see God.[1]

---

1. Matt 5:8.

Chapter 7

The Trust

THADDEUS WAS NOT WHO most people feared and held in contempt. There was someone else far more sinister than the emperor, one whose motivations and intentions were nothing less than totally depraved and destructive. Her role in the administration was to oversee the different oracles who made daily reports to the emperor about the affairs of the people who resided east of the empire.

The oracles were usually natives of the regions where they were assigned to monitor. This made it easier for them to blend into the community so that their role was not so obvious to other people. Their identities were usually unknown, but knowledge of their activities and the ramifications of their reports were widespread among the people. Therefore, people were often careful when speaking openly about the emperor since it was impossible to know whom to trust.

LUCIFER

Lucifer was one of Thaddeus's most trusted members of his administration. She worked her way to the top of the empire's ranks by sheer grit and persuasion. She had originally been a steward of ascetics and musical arts. Thaddeus loved the arts, perhaps more than the brutality of the arenas. He relished beautiful and calming expressions of poetry, music, and art.

It was Lucifer's responsibility to make sure the palace stayed adorned with the greatest artistic creations of all time. She knew their effect on the emperor and the long-term implications they had for her success in the administration. Nothing gained anyone more credibility than appeasing the emperor's palate for art and music. Lucifer fully invested herself in pleasing Thaddeus—whatever the price.

The price at times was costly. However, making herself sexually and sensually available was a small price to pay for advances to a position that controlled the emperor's perception of reality. Over the years, she learned to manipulate the news coming back from the oracles in a way that accomplished her aims. She intended to consume as much of Thaddeus's power and attention as possible. Lucifer had no boundaries of conscience. She epitomized greed and achievement at any cost.

Part of Lucifer's rise to power remained a mystery. No one knew much about her background or personal life. The details were sketchy. She became an orphan after her parents abandoned her as an infant. It is still unknown how Lucifer came to be placed at an orphanage that was run by the Roman administration, which turned out to be a fortunate situation. Consequently, she was tutored by the best teachers, scholars, and local clerics.

By the age of twelve, Lucifer mastered ten musical instruments and was a skilled painter beyond her years. Soon after her sixteenth birthday, she drew the attention of the administration. She received her first commission to sculpt the emperor's bust before reaching twenty years of age. Because she was female, Lucifer's accomplishments were almost unnoticed and not well documented.

Lucifer first caught the attention of the emperor while being pursued through the back roads near the palace. A group of royal soldiers intended to savagely assault her. Taller and more athletic than most of her male attackers, Lucifer overtook five of the assailants by killing them with her sword and shield. Then she mercilessly subdued the two remaining soldiers with her bare hands and braided ropes. The emperor was amazed at what he saw and ordered that Lucifer become a part of the palace's official security detail. This was a position she quickly excelled in and she soon became the principal lieutenant and Thaddeus's most trusted confidant.

"Permission to speak to the emperor?" asked Lucifer as she made an unexpected trip to the private palace of Thaddeus.

A guard stood at the gate entering the lower terrace. It was a cool evening. The sun had not set, but the clouds made the evening more tolerable.

"This is not your normal visitation time. Is everything alright?" questioned one of the guards. He was familiar with Lucifer and had often been captivated by her beauty.

"No, but I have urgent news for the emperor. My report should not wait until the regular time," Lucifer insisted.

The guards glanced at each other, one immediately recognizing the other's seniority, and dashed off to the inner chambers to gain permission to allow Lucifer to enter. It only seemed to take a few moments before the guard returned while Lucifer and the other guard stood in silence, never holding eye contact with each other. "Permission is granted. You may enter the courts," the senior uttered in a voice as if he was the one granting the permission. Lucifer appeared unimpressed as she proceeded toward the courtyard that led to the inner chamber.

Once at the entrance of the stone-covered room, Lucifer stood motionless, waiting for permission to speak. Thaddeus reclined across his chaise lounge of elaborate stone markings. She did not have to wait long for him to look in her direction and welcome her inside. Thaddeus was always excited to see her and to hear any news she reported about the murmurings in the streets.

"Lucifer, it is good to see you. As lovely as always. I don't know how you maintain such beauty," the emperor said.

Thaddeus felt free expressing his adoration to Lucifer after two glasses of evening wine and being aware that his wife was busy on the other side of the palace.

"Thank you, my lord, for your generous compliments and for taking the time to hear my report. Please forgive the unexpected appearance," Lucifer responded. She was careful not to react too strongly to the emperor's words. She was not as aware of the situation as Thaddeus was, therefore, she kept her behavior professional.

"My pleasure to do so. You are always welcomed here in my chamber." Thaddeus's attempts to flatter were effective even though a bit exaggerated.

"My lord, I come to make a report concerning the street performer known as Yeshua, who has been attracting crowds of over two hundred," Lucifer reported as she demonstrated her talent for exaggeration. However, it was true that the crowds were growing. "My lord, you know that my reports have always been accurate and truthful, and whatever I share with you is done so in the best interest of your kingdom."

Thaddeus was impressed by her words while also distracted by the multiple scenes of their past lovemaking racing through his mind. He fought to focus his attention on the preliminary statements.

Lucifer continued to speak, "Reports made by three of my oracles have substantiated the subversive activities of Yeshua in his dramas. One of which makes a direct statement disloyal to your kingship. I am here to apprise you of these subversive acts and advise a course of action."

"How serious should we take this? He is just a peasant street performer. What harm can he possibly bring to the empire?" Thaddeus asked as he grew impatient with the numerous suggestions that his status as a ruler could be so easily threatened. Lucifer sensed the emperor's annoyance but persisted.

"My lord, you are the incontestable leader of the empire and admired by all, but you cannot afford to allow even the slightest challenge to go unanswered," she said.

"So, what do you have to report?" Thaddeus answered.

Lucifer continued, "My lord. This street performer has created a character in his scenes he calls Jesus, the Greek form of his own name."

"I am aware of that. But what is in a name?" Thaddeus asked. "Who cares what language he uses?"

"He intends to attack not only your rule as emperor but our way of life," Lucifer replied. "One of these street acts was observed by my most trusted oracle. The character Jesus entered the sacred temple and started turning over tables and flogging the tax collectors with the very same whips used only by legion soldiers. He was protesting your handling of the Zealot uprising. For all we know, he is one of them. So you see, we cannot turn a blind eye to this man's performances."

"What was the crowd's response to this enactment?" Thaddeus probed.

Lucifer was not prepared for this line of questioning but quickly responded, "They applauded and cheered at the end," embellishing her report. There were no such definitive reports of the crowd's response. The oracle did not say how many people were even present. Lucifer had already decided that she had the emperor's attention and would not miss any opportunity to influence his decision by enhancing the details.

"So, what do you recommend I do about this?" Thaddeus was being savvy so as not to fully give in to Lucifer's wishes.

"Let me further investigate this Yeshua. I have someone who can find out more about him and his constituents. Give me thirty days to compile a full profile. I will make sure we have all the details needed to prove our case. This man may be more dangerous than we think," Lucifer said. Her confidence appeared to reassure Thaddeus.

"I hope you are wrong. Nevertheless, I will grant you permission. Give me time to draw up a warrant with my seal. I want this to be done the right way, so that I can maintain the respect and authority of the people," Thaddeus said firmly as to not appear to take such things less seriously than his predecessors.

Lucifer had anticipated Thaddeus's reaction. She already had in her possession a formal draft of the warrant with the details of who would carry out the investigation.

"My lord, I have saved you some time by preparing the order. All I need is your seal," she said while passing the scroll to Thaddeus's secretary.

Thaddeus always wore his seal on his right hand. It was a bronze ring specially designed for him with his signature stamp. A protected box for the emperor's wax seal rested on a table at the end of the lounge. He dipped the seal in the ink and stamped the warrant. "It is done. So be it."

"My lord. It is done," Lucifer gave one last sensual glance into the emperor's eye to assure him of her loyalty and continued availability. Thaddeus was tempted to take advantage of the moment, but he was not sure how long Petula would be in the west end.

THE WITNESSES

Sometime in late spring, Lucifer was busy finalizing the reports that had come in from across the region. As she reclined on the one-inch layer of soft padding that overlaid the stone chaise, her lips pressed tight as each written report was read from the rolls of papyri. The gaze of her eyes and the expression on her face indicated a sense of satisfaction.

I believe this will be enough information for the emperor to call for his death, she thought.

After reading the reports, Lucifer stood up. Her six-foot-five-inch frame commanded attention as she hurried to the front gate of her palace. There, a soldier waited with a chariot of two horses.

"Take me to the emperor's palace," she commanded. The soldier opened the side door of the chariot to allow Lucifer to be on the ground floor next to the soldier in charge. The soldier summoned the horses to gallop at a steady pace. Her facial expression was intense and focused as she stood slightly above the soldier in the chariot.

The ride to the emperor's palace went by in a flash. Fortunately, the sporadic rains had settled the dust on the roads, making them more accessible for transporting people in the city. Much of the pavement around the palace was recently laid, which enabled the sounds of the horses' feet to echo throughout the inner garden. The circle drive made it convenient when delivering VIP travelers wishing to enter the front entrance of the palace. By using this entrance, Lucifer moved quickly through the two chambers before reaching the main quarters of Thaddeus.

Lucifer tightly held the rolls of papyri in her hands as she entered Thaddeus's primary meeting room. He had already been notified of her arrival and was waiting for her to enter the room. Typically, reports were vetted at the governor's office. However, Thaddeus gave specific instructions that all matters related to Yeshua's performances be reported to his office directly. Lucifer's special relationship with Thaddeus allowed her access that no other officer in his cabinet had. As she walked into the room, they both looked each other in the eyes. They greeted each other with slight smiles that signaled that the images from the past were still alive in their minds.

"My lord. It is a great pleasure to see you on this day. I hope all is well with you," Lucifer spoke. It was customary for several members of the emperor's court to be present. Lucifer carefully kept the greeting formal and the salutations appropriate so as not to reveal the true nature of the relationship between them. "You are the only true leader of Rome. Your legacy will live on into eternity. I have traveled here to bring you my final report about the activities of the Judean called Yeshua, a raconteur of foolish fables. I beg my lord's permission to make my report plain to you."

"Lucifer, you are my trusted investigator. You may make your report in my presence. But only if there are at least two witnesses present. Do you have such?" Thaddeus announced with regal precision.

JUDAS THE ISCARIOT

"Yes, my lord. I have made special arrangements for these two witnesses to be present today. The first is Judas, the Iscariot," Lucifer announced as she ordered Judas to step forward. "He infiltrated the group of suspects by posing as an interested understudy. His witness is particularly important because of his firsthand knowledge of the planning of these subversive performances."

Lucifer was beaming with confidence and pride thanks to her successful plan to use Judas as a spy in her investigation.

"This is good to hear, but we must have him take the oath," Thaddeus ordered.

"Yes, my lord. I understand and will proceed," Lucifer responded and then turned toward Judas. "Judas of Iscariot. Will you raise your right hand toward the emperor?"

Judas, already standing at attention, raised his right hand. Lucifer then led him, word-for-word, through the official oath.

"I, Judas the Iscariot, do solemnly swear by the oath upon all gods, and in the presence of the lord of all lords, Emperor Thaddeus."

"I do my lord," said Judas.

Lucifer paused for dramatic effect, then proceeded with the oath, "That your testimony is true and reliable. That your employment by the emperor's supreme agent, Lucifer, and the standard payment of thirty pieces of silver, does not inhibit the veracity of your testimony or the accuracy of its intent. If you agree and swear, please state your name and repeat the words, 'By the mercy of the gods, I do.'"

Lucifer looked at Judas and paused for his response.

"I swear by the mercy of the gods and my lord," Judas repeated.

Lucifer continued her interrogation of Judas by saying, "Judas, you have been a part of the group of street performers, who go by the name The Ekklesia, led by the suspect in this investigation, Yeshua ben Samuel. These performances occur throughout the providence of Rome, mostly in the markets near and around the seaports. Is this true?"

"Yes, your honor," Judas responded.

"The crowds observing these performances have grown over time, especially after the creation of the fictitious character named Jesus. People have come to worship this character regardless of who performs the role. Is this also true?" she asked Judas. He responded with a nod and the same affirmative words he had given to her previous question.

Lucifer continued for some time with her carefully crafted descriptions and interrogations. Thaddeus was becoming impatient and weary of her interrogations and finally interrupted.

"This man is not on trial," Thaddeus said. "Discontinue this line of questioning and simply state the facts of what he knows."

Finally, she turned to Judas and asked, "Can you describe your involvement in this movement for our lord?"

"My lord," Judas slowly spoke. "I have worked with Yason, known to some as Yeshua, for almost two years. I was asked by Lucifer to provide information about his activities and the people's reactions. I performed in several scenes, always in a subservient role. Yason usually performed the role of Jesus. However, others also performed the role in smaller venues outside the main gate of the city. The crowds were always larger when Yason performed. In recent performances, more and more people have gathered around the marketplaces and the old temple grounds to see Yeshua. His dramas usually have a message of hope and redemption for the poor. Sometimes, there are so many people who come to watch that we have to turn them away. At the last performance, there must have been over a thousand people. The people love the man Jesus and his words of wisdom."

Lucifer interrupted with a question, "Do you think Yeshua used these performances to unite the Judean people? Is it true that they called him a messiah?"

"People called him many things. Some say that Yason is portraying the Jesus character as the coming Messiah," Judas answered. "I disagree. Jesus is like one of the prophets of old, but more gentile in his ways. Often in the stories, Jesus makes friends with gentiles, pagans, and sinners. I don't believe messiahs would associate with such people. It seems that Yason is trying to unite all people, not just Judeans. Most of his scenes are offensive to any self-respecting Judean."

Judas paused in anticipation of the next question.

"So, answer the question," Lucifer continued. "Does this Jesus character show dishonor to the emperor?"

"Not so," Judas carefully answered. "Many of the performances dishonor our religious leaders. Also, he uses words that refer to the coming reign of Israel's god." Judas paused to think. He looked down at the ground. "In one particular scene, Jesus does refer to himself as a son of god."

"Really!" Lucifer said with excitement. "So, he does claim to be a son of a god. Everyone knows that there is only one true son of god." Lucifer turned to the emperor. "My lord, you have heard it for yourself. The man dishonors your name by constructing this character named Jesus who makes false and threatening claims to be a son of a god!"

Judas interjected, usurped Lucifer's role as mediator, and spoke directly to the emperor, "My lord, there is one thing you must know."

Thaddeus finally broke his silence, "And what is that?"

"Jesus will die in the next act," Judas said.

"Die? Then he cannot be a son of god. A son of god would never die. His legacy would live forever, and his message would be alive in the hearts of men," Thaddeus explained. Hearing the ephemeral nature of Yeshua's performances gave some relief to the emperor's concerns.

Lucifer spoke again, "I told you, my lord. The character Jesus is only a deciduous projection of Yeshua's imagination. He is no real threat to your throne, but he must be made an example for the people."

She then returned to questioning Judas. "So, do you have any idea how Jesus will die in the next production?" She inquired.

Judas was reluctant to give details. However, he knew his credibility with the emperor would be in jeopardy if he discovered information was being withheld.

"He will be arrested and executed by the Roman government," Judas said as he lowered the tone of his voice.

"What!" Thaddeus was appalled by this revelation. "How dare Yeshua be so presumptuous. No one will be permitted to circumscribe the actions of the Roman government. He will be arrested immediately. Let it be done."

Lucifer interrupted again, "But my lord, you cannot arrest a man for something he has not yet done. Please, I beg you, allow Judas to continue his work for now. When the time comes, I will arrange for him to be captured in the act. He will be taken into custody even as he performs on the stage, humiliated in front of his followers."

Thaddeus, who was angered from the previous testimony, paused to think carefully about Lucifer's request. He looked at her directly, but he was not able to gaze at her without giving into wild fantasies. Thaddeus had become a prisoner of her passions. Without much resistance or hesitation, he conceded to her wishes.

"Do as you must. Just bring him to me," he ordered.

Lucifer moved swiftly to present to Thaddeus the orders for his seal. She had carefully crafted the words so that any soldier would know to only arrest Yeshua after he performs the death of Jesus. She also directed Judas to return to the rehearsals.

"Make sure you do not disclose this information to anyone," Lucifer warned Judas. "We have all that we need to bring him in. If you do anything to alert him to our intentions, I will have your head on a stick and no pieces of silver for you."

"I understand fully. You can trust me," Judas reassured Lucifer. "The next rehearsal will take place in a few days. I will report back to you as soon as I learn the exact time and place of the next performance."

Thaddeus questioned Lucifer, "Where is your second witness?"

Lucifer immediately responded, "I have not vetted her yet. Her name is Alexia, the daughter of one of your constituents. I know exactly where to find her."

Chapter 8

The Rehearsal

YESHUA LOVED BEING WITH Alexia, and Alexia loved being with Yeshua, but no one could know about their love nor their clandestine encounters. As long as Yeshua was under the careful eye of the Roman government and Alexia was the daughter of a Roman official, their love could never be. However, the love between them grew stronger as time passed.

On a chilly spring morning, they managed to steal a few moments alone. Alexia had ordered her custodians to run an errand. For several reasons, their time was limited. First, being together in any one place for an extended time increased the risk of being discovered. Second, Alexia's father was very protective. Although she could leave the palace from time to time, questions about her whereabouts occurred if gone for too long. Trips with her escorts were short so as not to arouse the suspicions of her father.

Yeshua usually spent the mornings preparing for rehearsals by reviewing each line aloud to himself. He needed to complete his rehearsal before the Sabbath began. That day, he prepared for the death of Jesus. He thought long and hard about how to portray him. Alexia had grown increasingly worried about Yeshua. Rumors about his activities had increased in the palace. The word came to her father that the Romans planned to put an end to his performances.

"I am worried about you," Alexia whispered in Yeshua's ear as they reclined at his father's compound.

Yeshua's two-room brick house, which he built for himself, was located on the far east side of his father's farm. Its remote location afforded him the luxury of escaping from the main events at the compound's center. It was also far enough away from the pig pens that the smell was often not detectable. His place was on the edge of the farm, nestled among the trees, and it gave them the privacy needed to relax and enjoy quality time.

"Don't worry about me. Everything will be fine," Yeshua tried to convince Alexia, but it was not working.

"Have you decided how Jesus will die?" Realizing she would not get the assurances she needed from Yeshua, Alexia switched the subject to something less intense.

"Yes, I have given careful consideration for how I want the death to occur," Yeshua said.

Alexia moved closer to Yeshua, who was now leaning back against the wall of his cottage. She sat down next to him and leaned her head against his chest.

"I hope it is not too violent. He is so adored by so many of your followers. You do not want him to die a shameful death," Alexia said.

Yeshua paused to contemplate Alexia's suggestion. "I understand that. But I also want his death to be meaningful. So, I have decided to construct a series of events that will correlate with the Passover feast," he explained.

Alexia interrupted, "What? Why Passover? You are going to offend people."

Yeshua quickly sought to justify his plan. "I thought about that. People think of Jesus as this divine person. Some compare him to the Messiah. He is not a god who comes to rescue people from the oppression of their enemies. He is one of the people. That is what I want people to see and to feel in their hearts. That he is one of them, and that his death will serve as an example of what happens to anyone who questions Roman rule."

"So, how will you show them this?" Alexia asked.

"First, the opening scene will be Jesus riding into the old town on the back of an ass," Yeshua explained.

Alexia stopped him again. "You mean the prophecy of Zechariah? The legend of the coming of the Messiah, who will arrive in humility, riding on an ass, and reclaim the throne of David?"

"Yes, that is true," Yeshua said. "But instead of riding into the heart of the old city, Jesus will be arrested by the Romans and put to death by execution for claiming to be a ruler like Thaddeus."

"This is insane! You will offend the priests and anger the Romans with this performance. The authorities will arrest you for this," Alexia said as she became frightened for him. Her voice became loud and her expression more intense. "I don't see how anything good can come of this."

"It shows the conspiracy between the government and our so-called leaders. Jesus is a threat to their cozy alliance. He exposes their deeds for what they truly are," Yeshua said.

Yeshua continued to try to help Alexia understand. "We both knew the Judean leaders have no authority to execute a person. Only the Roman authorities will put Jesus to death. It will take three actors to perform the short act. One would be Jesus and another person in the role of the Roman soldier. And the last character would be someone who will act as the governor."

"Oh no, that will infuriate Simon the governor if you do that," Alexia said, reminding Yeshua of what he should have already known.

"I know, my love. I do not wish to incite the governor's anger. Nevertheless, the truth is the truth. The governor is supposed to represent the interests of the people. He is one of us, and Judah runs through his veins. Instead of placing the needs of the people first, he has laid in bed with the Romans. They pay him to do their bidding. His idolatry must be exposed for what it is."

"I trust your judgment," Alexia held tightly to Yeshua's hand. "You are all I care about. I love you more than anything else in this world. If they come for you, I will be ready. I have already paid for the boat that will take us away from here. We have nothing to worry about."

Yeshua pulled Alexia closer to him as she rested her head in the middle of his chest. The sound of his heart echoed through her ears.

"I love you and trust you the same," said Yeshua. "We shall be together on the other side of the river. Surely, the emperor will come for me. I know this will be the case, but I must tell the truth about our oppression. I am willing to make the necessary sacrifice to see justice in the land."

Yeshua held Alexia tightly as he firmly pressed his lips against hers for what seemed like an eternity. It was only a matter of time. If it were later in the day when the sun sets, then they would have made love. Soon, however, the other actors would be arriving to rehearse for the next performance, so Alexia pulled away from Yeshua's kiss for the moment.

"I will leave you for now. I will be waiting for you as we have planned," Alexia said as she rose and headed for the doorway. "May the blessing of Abraham be with you, my love."

After Alexia left, Yeshua remained on the floor in a daze. He thought about how much he wanted to make love with Alexia. Then he returned to thinking about and planning the next scene before the others arrived for rehearsal.

Those performing closer to the inner-city courts would draw a different reaction from the crowds than those acting on the city's outskirts. Yeshua was careful not to plan the performances too close in proximity so that one audience's responses would not interfere with those of other audiences.

Yeshua identified four areas of the province based on regions where Yeshua's performances had become widely accepted. The northern area embraced the narratives' philosophical themes, while the southern part preferred the arrangements' religious themes. Yeshua hoped that the simultaneous performances create a cataclysmic evolution throughout Rome, resulting in a transformation across the regions.

THE REHEARSAL BEGINS

As midday slowly approached, Yeshua grew eager to meet with the actors to rehearse the death of Jesus. After much discussion and debate, everyone agreed that Jesus should die at the hands of the Romans.

The standard method of crucifixion, using cross beams and nails, seemed too brutal for the stage. Crucifixion by the Romans was usually public and cruel. Large nails were often pierced through the victim's wrists and ankles, resulting in suffocation by asphyxiation.

Yeshua intentionally modified the Roman crucifixion method so that it became a far cry from the more gruesome Philistine executions of ancient times, but it was still staged in such a way as to convey its humiliation and suppression of basic human dignity. Yeshua's reconstruction produced an equally dramatic effect without the barbarism.

As the actors arrived at Yeshua's home, the death scene was met with nascent trepidation by some. Yeshua, Petras, James, and Yohanan would perform in the next production. Extras would fill peripheral parts like the crowds and the role of Simon the governor.

"I now summon the attention of you all," Yeshua raised his voice to bring quiet in the room. "The death of Jesus will occur this way. After riding into the city on an ass, the crowds will scream in excitement. To ensure the reaction of the crowds, I have asked several of our supporters to place themselves among the audiences. They will encourage the crowds to participate in the performance. We tried this several months ago and it proved to be an effective method."

Petras then spoke, "Yason, what if the crowds do not participate? Some will truly think that you are making a mockery of the ancient prophets."

Yeshua responded, "That is a risk I am willing to take. The people who follow us are not traditionalists. They are not captive to the old ways. Most are ready for new ideas and new ways of thinking about the world." He continued with the rehearsal. "As Jesus enters the city gates, two Roman soldiers will arrest him immediately for claiming to be a king. To do this we have uniforms sewn by our friends, Martha and Mary, who are known for their sartorial designs. They are not exact to design, but close enough to be recognized as imperial garments."

Thomas, who would be portraying a Roman soldier, questioned Yeshua. "Yason, there will be actual Roman soldiers around who will not allow such counterfeit displays. Is it not against civil law to impersonate a soldier?"

"Yes. You are right, but our soldiers will not bear the emperor's seal." Yeshua continued. "During the arrest, there will be no dialogue. Our actions will interpret the meaning of the event. Jesus will immediately be led away toward the stage where the governor appears."

Yeshua recalled in his mind what Alexia said about offending the governor. He admired her honor and respect for authority and its potential benefits for their relationships. He also knew that including Simon's role would draw attention to the years of exploiting the people by one of their own. The governor was one of the most hated leaders in the province. Some hated him more than the emperor himself.

Petras spoke again, "Yason, may I suggest the trial scene focus on Jesus's relationship with God, the prophets, and his obedience to God's will?"

"The governor does not care anything about obedience to God's will," responded Yeshua. "It is power that he cares about. Jesus's claim to power and authority is his greatest concern. His claims to be a king are the only thing that will get him killed. I want to try something very different this time," he said to them.

Everyone listened intently. Any sudden change usually created anxiety among the participants, but Yeshua's mellifluous voice often put everyone at ease.

Yeshua continued, "I call it simultaneous performances."

"What is this simultaneous performance?" Yohanan asked.

Yeshua answered, "We will conduct multiple performances of the same narrative at the same time in different parts of the province. Hence, simultaneous performances."

James, the elder brother of Yeshua, puzzled by the announcement, said, "Interesting idea. What purpose will these simultaneous performances accomplish?"

Yeshua had anticipated this question and had already thought about his explanation. "As you know by now, the Roman authorities have been closely watching us. They have done this in several ways. Sometimes there are soldiers on guard. Other times there are Roman informants in the crowds. Immediately following a performance, these individuals report directly back to Simon the governor, whether our dramas are divisive or disruptive. Their reports about one performance directly impact the response to the next performance of the same act. The rumors and opinions about one performance which circulate among the people affect how the next production is received. By performing the same scene simultaneously, we will prevent these rumors and opinions from getting out before the next performance."

The men looked at Yeshua and then at each other, nodding in agreement with the logic of Yeshua's explanation. They not only agreed with his reasoning but were fascinated by his brilliance and forward-thinking attitude. Yeshua was like a military commander in their minds, planning strategies to combat the enemy by accurately anticipating their next step. It was precisely the reason why Yeshua had gained their respect and trust. Yeshua's plan for simultaneous performances was not merely for strategic reasons to control publicity. Unbeknownst to them, Yeshua's next production had the potential of provoking a response from the Roman authorities that could jeopardize each of their well-being. Yeshua had been planning patiently for the right moment to cross the boundary between harmless political satire and intentional disregard of governmental authority.

The rehearsal lasted late into the night. The men continued to question Yeshua about each scene. Although they all agreed with Yeshua that Jesus must die, they also understood the risk involved. They were afraid of what could happen if the Roman soldiers intervened. So much was at stake for them. Yeshua was insistent that Jesus must die. After the governor's trial, Jesus would be handed over to the Roman soldiers for execution. Yeshua, Petras, James, and Yohanan would play the principal role of Jesus.

"Once Jesus is in the custody of the soldiers, the governor will proceed with his interrogation," Yeshua explained. "I have carefully selected these questions to show the true intent of the governor. It will be clear that he doesn't want to get his hands dirty in the matter. He will specifically ask Jesus whether he is a king or not. Jesus will only respond by saying, 'You say that I am?' The governor will grow increasingly frustrated until he finally turns Jesus over to the Roman soldiers."

BROKEN TRUST

While Yeshua described the scene leading to the death of Jesus, Judas suddenly walked into the rehearsal space through a back entryway. He quietly found a place in the back corner of the room. By then, nightfall had settled, and the brisk cool air of spring began blowing through the open windows. A fire was lit in a wood basin in the middle of the room and gave a faint orange glow.

All others sat on the floor in a circle around the fire. Yeshua stood in the middle of the room. His eyes caught a glimpse of Judas as he moved to stand along the back wall. Yeshua decided not to acknowledge his presence, nor did he question why he was late for the rehearsal. Ordinarily, Yeshua scolded those who arrived late for rehearsals. But this time, he sensed that Judas was intentional about not wanting to be noticed, which seemed strange to Yeshua.

After the arrival of Judas, Yeshua became more cautious about his descriptions of the final scene. He carefully chose each word. The assiduous descriptions of the arrest of Jesus painted a vivid picture of the movements leading up to the trial. Judas sat and listened carefully for each detail narrated by Yeshua. Reporting the important facts back to Lucifer would be crucial in planning their actions against Yeshua.

The more Judas listened, the more he was reminded of his admiration for Yeshua. Suddenly feelings of remorse flooded his conscience. *What have I done?* The words echoed through Judas's mind as he sat in silence. *Please forgive me for what I am going to do.* He hoped his silence would not reveal his guilt. It unexpectedly began to storm.

Spring storms always brought fresh rain for the verdant plant life in the countryside. The rain against the roof made it more challenging to hear Yeshua's words. Judas was relieved by the distraction of the thunder and rain. Judas considered leaving to go and pretend to bathe in the rain. As soon as he conceded to the thought, Yeshua's eyes gazed directly at Judas.

FAMILY TRUST

Just as Yeshua was about to begin rehearsing the next scene, Miriam entered the room from the east entrance. It surprised Yeshua since his mother seldom came to his abode. She had been meticulous not to interrupt his rehearsals. Judas was equally startled by her appearance. He imagined the possibility that Miriam had learned about his activities and was coming to warn the others.

She brought three large baskets with her and she struggled to lift them. She carried one on each shoulder and balanced the third on her head. The sight was comical. Yeshua had never seen his mother perform domestic tasks like his father's hired servants.

"It is getting so late. The storms are getting stronger. You all need to stop and eat something," said Miriam.

She set down each basket and opened their lids. Each item of food was subject to the traditional ablution rituals. Miriam was careful not to reveal her true intentions to her son's guests. Her visit had little to do with food or the vicinal location of Yeshua's hut on the family's compound. The conversation between Samuel and Josephus still lingered in her mind. She was afraid in her heart about what might happen to Yeshua if his actions continued to agitate the emperor. She needed to come, see, and hear for herself about the next performance. Food was only a convenient decoy for her true motivations. She kneeled on the ground, reached into each basket, revealed the contents of bread, spices, fresh meats, and wine.

"So, Yason, you have been working for a long time tonight. This next performance must be something really important to you," Miriam probed as she divided the various food items and arranged them succinctly on the cloths covering the ground. "You have been so quiet about this performance. Usually, you tell me about your stories. But I have not heard you say anything about this one."

The others remained silent and refused to take the bait to share their leader's intentions. Each one stayed in their place and waited for the distribution of the food and drink among them. Martha and Yael quickly rushed to Miriam's side to assist in setting out the food.

Meanwhile, Yeshua was formulating in his mind a discreet response to his mother's inquiry.

Should I tell her the truth?

He pondered the repercussions of disclosing the final scene to his mother. She did not know about the plot to kill the character named Jesus. Like others, Miriam had come to adore Jesus. She found him to be inspirational and empowering. As one of Yeshua's most faithful followers, his mother attended almost every performance. She eagerly waited for the right time to provide motherly feedback. It was peculiar for Yeshua not to have already discussed the next act with her.

Yeshua finally spoke, "Mother, I have been so busy. Since father increased my responsibilities on the farm there has not been enough time in the day to recount the details to you."

Miriam showed no indication that Yeshua's excuse deterred her from inquiring about the next production. She continued to place the food and wine in their appropriate places.

"That is no excuse for not talking to your mother," she said. "You have always been a busy young man and unfailingly into tasks that consume your time. Yet, you have always found time to spend with your mother."

She attempted to try a different, more passive-aggressive approach to get the information she wanted from Yeshua.

"If you do not want to tell me about your next performance, that is fine with me. You are a man of age, capable of making your own decisions, and I will respect your privacy," Miriam said.

Miriam's change in deposition seemed to work. She realized that others in the room might have heard their conversation. Although it was an honorable thing to do, Yeshua resisted telling his mother the truth.

Yeshua finally grabbed his mother's free arm to draw her close enough to whisper, "Mother, I will tell you about the next performance, but right now we need to continue with the rehearsal. You and I will talk about it later when we are alone. After we finish tonight, I will come to see you. The hour is getting late, and we must practice our lines."

Yeshua spoke with a more respectful tone, which was a blatant attempt to be more effective. He desperately needed her to leave to save face among his performers. He looked directly at her. "Please do not argue with me this time."

Miriam understood the look on her son's face. She had seen the same expression many times on her husband's face when he desperately needed her to comply. It was vital for her to display a public show of respect among outside observers. She knew all too well the personal consequences of not cooperating.

"That would be fine with me. I will wait for you," Miriam said as she finished the extensive arrangements of food and wine.

The storms were now gone, and the rains ceased. Miriam proceeded to leave through the same entrance she came in. "I will be waiting for you," she said once more while walking out of the hut.

At last, Yeshua could finish rehearsal without interruption. However, he knew that rehearsing tonight would be impossible after devouring the food and wine. Besides, there was no real way to know for sure if his mother had hidden outside to listen to the rehearsal.

Yeshua accepted that rehearsal was over, sat down between Petras and Yohanan by the fire, and prepared to serve the meal. He felt relieved to finally have some time with his trusted companions. Many of them were eager to hear about the final scene. Judas continued to contemplate leaving, but he decided that doing so would only draw more attention to himself.

While serving each one, Yeshua spoke, "Before we partake in this meal together, I would like to lead us in a blessing."

The others in the room slowly gathered closer, in a circle, to listen to Yeshua. Although he was not an expressively religious person, Yeshua relished their tradition's religious rituals' dramatic performance. The actors all sat on the ground around Yeshua as he arose and looked intensely at the group. Often his presence spoke louder than his words. In this instance, both the anticipation of his blessing and the towering of his physical body captured their attention, as if he were announcing a new religious commandment. After a few moments of silence, Yeshua began his prayer:

> *Holy One of the Ages, blessed be your name among all names,*
> *Please abide with us, now and forever.*[1]
> *Your reign shall be done on earth as it is in the heavens,*
> *We need so many things from you,*
> *feed us with words of wisdom,*
> *as you have provided for our daily bread,*
> *bless the hands of the one who has prepared our meal,*
> *do not allow our sins or the sins of others to impede us,*
> *curse anyone who betrays our trust,*
> *forgive us for not always being reflections of your grace,*
> *Remove any temptations from our paths,*
> *but lead us down the path of righteousness and justice,*
> *May your divine peace abide in the hearts of all*
> *who have committed themselves to this work,*
> *For you are all that we need*
> *Aman.*

Everyone responded with the customary "Aman," usually a sign of mutual agreement, but for some, it was an affirmation of their common fate.

"Let us prepare to eat. There are basins of freshwater in the back," Yeshua said.

The last time that they rehearsed Yeshua included a traditional footwashing before the meal. However, Petras caused such a loud uproar about its appropriateness, Yeshua decided not to resurrect the issue at that time.

"There is plenty for everyone. So, feel free to indulge yourselves," he said.

Yael, one of the few women present at the rehearsal, took keen observations of Judas' behavior. She decided to say something to Yeshua in case it had escaped his attention. When to say something proved to be more complicated than she expected. Several people were trying to talk to Yeshua before the meal began. She was often paralyzed by the traditional gender expectations that dictated women to wait for permission to speak. Waiting for such an opportune time may never happen amidst the frenzy of other male counterparts bidding for a chance to offer their opinions about the next performance.

---

1. Matt 6:9–13.

Chapter 9

Betrayal

A FEW WEEKS BEFORE the simultaneous performances, the members of The Ekklesia gathered at Yeshua's home to share a meal and discuss the final preparations. There was plenty of fish, bread, and wine. In the hut, each person reclined on individual pallets to enjoy the deliciously prepared food. Miriam was well-known for her meals and often entertained the guests who came to visit her husband.

The women in the room sat together in their own space on the floor near the eastside entrance. They engaged in a lively discussion about their hopes and dreams for the future and some conversation about the changing social norms of Galilean life. There was some chatter and laughter about a rumor going around about Yeshua seeing the daughter of a well-known Roman elitist, but they soon dismissed those speculations.

"That is insane," one of the women said. The others laughed at the idea.

Yeshua and the men also conversed about politics and social conditions. Petras was the most vocal of the group.

"Times are hard for our people," he said. "The rich are getting richer, and the poor are dying in the streets. Only the merchants and wealthy farmers are surviving these times. Something needs to change. We cannot just dream and wait for a messiah to save us. We must save ourselves with God's help."

Petras spoke loudly, and the other men concurred with various grunts. As they talked, the wine continued to disembogue from their wineskins. Just as he was about to speak, Thomas's wine started leaking slowly on to the ground. Marco noticed it and began to laugh aloud as he pointed to the place of the leak.

Yeshua laughed and said, "That's why you never put new wine in old wineskins."

He and the others burst out into fierce collective laughter. Although they were all drunk, the symbolism was clear to them all. Galilean life had become a mixture of old Judean traditions and new cultural influences. Commerce and trade in the region had divided the haves and the have-nots and pitted families and neighbors against one another. The solution to the divide seemed out of reach. Yeshua believed that the Jesus character should reflect the political and cultural divide, and his death would serve as a small attempt to bridge the gap.

As the evening ended, midnight approached and the wineskins were all empty. Yeshua rose to his feet while he held a chalice of wine in his right hand and a loaf of bread in his left. It had been their custom for the host to end the meal with a blessing for the guests. He stumbled at first to stand straight; the expression on his face appeared as if he was waking up from a long sleep.

He stood in the middle of the room while the others remained seated. Yeshua offered a blessing,

> To all of you, my friends, I offer this blessing. May you all re-
> member this moment as an opportunity to make a difference in
> the lives of our people. I hold this cup of new wine up as a symbol
> of the new world order. May we all commit ourselves to this op-
> portunity to make a change for the better.

Yeshua held his chalice of wine up high in the air. As wine spilled out, he opened his mouth to catch the drops. In his drunken state, he missed several that landed in his beard. Others in the room followed his lead and did the same with varying levels of success. Judas chose not to participate, merely watching the others and hoping to go unnoticed.

Yeshua then held up one of the leftover loaves of bread,

> Also, take this loaf of bread for the nourishment of your bod-
> ies. May the stories we tell help nourish the minds and hearts
> of a new generation of Judeans and Greeks who want to work
> together to build a new future.

Yeshua took the loaf of bread, divided it, and distributed the rest of it around the room. Again, Judas quickly passed the bread to his left when it was his turn. Yeshua noticed. At first, he thought to dismiss Judas's behavior, but his mind was telling him differently. He remembered Judas's actions at the previous rehearsals—the way he stood outside the circle of the other actors. So, Yeshua decided to say something regardless of how others received it in the room. But he instinctively knew that if he allowed Judas to go unchallenged that it would jeopardize his credibility among the others.

"Judas," Yeshua said as his eyes fixed on him, "Is there some reason why you are not eating and drinking with us. Does our drunkenness offend you? Tell me, brother, what is the problem?"

Judas thought long and hard. Never had he felt so exposed in the group. The room suddenly became still and motionless. All eyes were fixed on Judas, waiting anxiously to hear what he had to say. The flames from the firepit gave his complexion an ominous color like the desert sand at sunset. Judas's mind raced to find adequate words, but nothing crystalized. His response needed to sound convincing without a logy tone. But nothing came to mind. He felt empty and exposed.

"Nothing is wrong, Yeshua, my friend," Judas finally spoke. It was the best he could do at the time. Hopefully, it helped stall the conversation until he could think of something better to say. The lack of available words was surprising to Judas, who prided himself on being a polyglot. "I am just lost in my thoughts about the upcoming performance," Judas said in a lower voice with his eyes looking downward. The explanation seemed to ease the tension between them, but Yeshua did not let Judas off the hook so quickly.

"Really. And what were you thinking about that consumed you so much? We are all listening," Yeshua asked sarcastically.

Judas was stunned. He had not anticipated such an inquisition. Again, he found himself at a loss for words. Now his heart began to pound deep in his chest. There was no way to rescue himself from this dilemma. Visions of Lucifer confronting him about allowing himself to be exposed began to populate his consciousness. Considering the possibility of having to face her overwhelmed him more than being called out by Yeshua. Besides, he liked Yeshua and believed in his cause. He hated Lucifer, but she offered thirty pieces of silver. Yeshua had been his motivation for a new vision of the world and himself. He needed to decide, and he needed to make it quickly before his silence broke the trust between Yeshua and himself. No longer able to contain himself.

Judas spoke, "Yason, I have something I must confess."

"You have something you need to tell us?" Yeshua repeated.

Yeshua delighted in the possible confirmation of what he already suspected. More than that, forcing Judas to show his true self thrilled Yeshua in unanticipated ways.

"We welcome your confession. Please share with us what you have to say," Yeshua spoke in a calm tone that was a betrayal of the anger building inside him.

Judas nervously told in detail how he had been reporting back to Lucifer the activities of the group. He confessed to it all. He tried to explain why he betrayed them.

"Yason, I believe in you and The Ekklesia," he said. "I did not want to bring harm to this mission. At first, your actions posed no threat to the emperor. So, my reports were not taken seriously. I became dependent on their compensation. The more they gave me, the more information they expected. I did not know that your performances were going to disturb the emperor to the point of your arrest. I just wanted to make a few denarii before our final performance." By now, Judas was frantically speaking faster, tears flowed down his cheeks, and the feelings of anguish distorted his face.

"Please, I beg you all, I did not plan for things to get so out of control. Yeshua, I beg your forgiveness and understanding," he pleaded with Yeshua.

"I should kill you where you stand," Petras emphatically said, knowing that they were all pacifists.

"I agree," said Yohanan, not wishing to appear less committed than Petras.

"I never meant to hurt anyone," Judas yelled in his defense. "Lucifer came to me. A while ago, I was arrested for laundering. The penalty was a severe jail sentence. So, I pleaded with Lucifer and promised to do whatever so that she would not send me to jail. I was released and allowed to return home. I did not hear anything for many days. After she found out I was assisting with the performances, I was summoned to the palace. I agreed to report about the narratives and information about where the next performances were to occur. Lucifer offered money for my efforts. I did not think much would come of it. You must believe me!" Judas pleaded.

Suddenly Petras lunged toward Judas and screamed, "I will kill you myself, and we both will burn in hell." A kerfuffle broke out in the room as the others tried to restrain Petras from what appeared to be his attempt to strangle Judas. "Let me go!" Petras insisted. Judas quickly moved toward the entrance to escape.

"Judas, where are you going?" Yeshua asked. Judas stood motionless.

"I am sorry, Yason, for betraying your trust and the trust of the others. I did not mean to bring harm to any of you," Judas said in a low, solemn voice. He bowed his head in a way that reminded Yeshua of the humility that he first admired upon meeting Judas. Also, it made him think about how camels are trained to bow down in order to enter the east gate of the city—commonly called the "eye of the needle." The camels signified the presence of foreigners bringing the exotic spices used with the pork meats sold from his father's farm—always a welcomed sight.

"I forgive you, Judas, for you know not what you did," Yeshua said, hoping to convince Judas to stay.

Judas briefly looked up at Yeshua, but he said nothing. He turned around again, facing the exit, and quickly entered the darkness of the night.

The others stood watching as Judas departed. Some were still clutching Petras, who struggled desperately to break free from their grip. Finally, after it was clear that Judas was gone and not returning, they released their hold on Petras. Petras turned around and pushed against the chest of Thomas, who led the efforts to restrain him. The wine was now wearing off, allowing men and women to think more clearly. The knowledge that Lucifer was aware of the next performance was sobering to all of them.

Martha stood next to Yeshua. "What should we do, Yason?" she questioned. "We cannot perform as planned. It is now too risky." The others in the room nodded in agreement. There appeared to be a consensus that their plans must change.

"We will proceed as planned," Yeshua said. "If the emperor were going to arrest us, he would have done so by now. I do not believe Judas would betray us by telling Lucifer about the next performance."

Thomas spoke, "Are you sure about that, Yason? I don't trust him. He is probably on his way to the palace as we speak. We should all flee to the old city and hide from the soldiers. They will be coming for us."

"Thomas, where is your faith?" Yeshua moved across the room toward him. He cautiously pulled back the corner of the window covering to peek outside. "The night is getting long, and the village is quiet. If they were coming, we would have heard them."

Yeshua's words did not reassure everyone in the room. The women were usually more trusting than the men. They all could see the anxiety on each other's faces. For now, all they could do was to wait and pray.

The betrayal by Judas drove a wedge between the members of The Ekklesia. Many considered Judas's role in the group unnecessary. There were more essential elements that needed their attention if the simultaneous performances were to be successful. After Judas vacated the room, a peace settled among those who remained. The real challenge before them was to maintain cohesiveness, something Yeshua had become accustomed to doing. Most of them trusted in Yeshua's faith more than they did their own.

"Put your trust in me and I will not lead you astray," Yeshua assured them.

"We put our trust in you," they all responded in unison.

THE SECOND WITNESS

The following morning Yeshua woke up before the sun rose. His head was throbbing—still consumed by the events of the previous night. Still fresh upon his palate, the wine took several moments to awaken his body and help him realize he was not dreaming. Scenes of Judas's confession and Petras's attempted assault, a syzygy of events, remained hazy. Everything seemed to unravel as the night progressed.

Yeshua stood naked in his room. He gazed out the window and wondered how he had become entangled in his current circumstances. He began to have moments of doubt and questioning. What if he had never started having street performances? What if he had kept them satirical and had not provided political commentary? Was it too late to change the course of events? Could Judas be trusted? All these questions polluted Yeshua's judgment about the final performance and his estimation about whether or not to proceed.

If the repercussions only involved Yeshua, then the answer to these questions would be simple. However, an argument could be made for Yeshua's propitious leadership. After all, the other actors sought him out—he did not choose them. These thoughts not only confused Yeshua, but they distracted him from the original omphalos of the act's subject.

The character Jesus consumed the performances in ways that Yeshua never intended. For this reason, Yeshua had come to resent the man Jesus, the character who captivated the imagination of the people but who had hijacked the foundational message—that all people are equal in God's sight. There were to be no heroes in the liberation struggle. That was the truth that Yeshua always wanted to be at the forefront of the performances.

As Yeshua pondered the next course of action and dressed for the day's work, the sound of footsteps echoed from a distance. Right away, Yeshua recognized the cadence of Alexia's steps among those of her escorts. Her footsteps' tempo sounded desperate and fast, not entirely running, but fast enough to signal urgency. Yeshua looked outside his window and confirmed it was her.

Alexia's pace increased as she came closer to the entrance of Yeshua's home. Her face displayed an unusual panic that Yeshua had never seen before. The look dispelled any presumption that Alexia was moving fast because she was enthusiastic about seeing him. It was evident that she had something else on her mind.

"Yason, it is me, Alexia," she shouted as she approached his entryway.

Yeshua stood in the doorway, having only his hips covered with clothing. Any other day, Alexia would have immediately undressed him at the entrance. Something different was on her mind, and it seemed that she did not notice his unbridled clothing.

"My love. It is too early for you to be here. Is something wrong?" Yeshua asked.

"Yason. Judas is dead," Alexia whispered so as to not alarm Yeshua, knowing it would not likely work.

"Dead!" Yeshua responded. "What do you mean by this?"

Alexia proceeded to explain. "Yes, Judas is dead. My father told me this morning. He said Judas was to report back to Lucifer by daybreak, but he never showed up. So, Lucifer sent the soldiers to find him. They searched for him most of the morning."

"Sit down here, my love," Yeshua held Alexia's hand as he guided her to the floor.

As she sat down next to him, Yeshua placed both arms around Alexia as she continued to tell him about Judas' death.

"The soldiers found him running through a field on the edge of the valley toward the mountains," Alexia told him.

No doubt Judas counted on the submontane landscape to provide a shield for his escape. They subdued him and brought him back to the palace to face Lucifer. After questioning him for hours into the evening, Judas refused to tell Lucifer about the final performance. She ordered him to be flogged and taken to the market square for execution. When dawn approached, and the sun rose in the eastern sky, Judas had been crucified and stripped of his clothes. Soldiers remained at the foot of the cross to tell people who passed, "This will be the fate of anyone who mocks the emperor's authority."

"What did your father have to say about his execution?" Yeshua asked.

"He told me he had heard things about us. He wanted to warn me that this was an example of what happened to people who associated themselves with you. He knew that Judas was an associate of yours and was reporting to Lucifer about your performances," Alexia explained.

"And what did you say to your father about us?"

"I told him I had only witnessed one of your performances. But I don't think he believed me. He continued to warn me not to have anything to do with you. And if I did, your fate would be the same as Judas," Alexia spoke while intermittently crying.

Yeshua thought long and hard about the things he heard from Alexia. He wondered what she was feeling and thinking about him. What was going to be their next move? Would she remain by his side or retreat to the safety of her father's house?

Meanwhile, Yeshua grew concerned about the safety of his mother and father. He had not heard anything from his parents since his mother brought the food for their meal. Suddenly the wine in his stomach started to come alive and caused him to say things that he did not necessarily mean.

"Alexia. You must leave me and never return. You are not safe with me," Yeshua shouted.

Alexia began to cry more profusely. "Yason, I will never leave you. My life is with you and I will never part from you. I don't care about being safe. I will die with you if I have to."

Yeshua delighted in the reaffirmation of Alexia's words. It was what he wanted her to say but did not know how to ask her.

He then said, "I will never let anything happen to you. So, we must leave this place as we planned to do. The simultaneous performances will occur as planned. Yohanan and Petras know exactly what to do. They know that we will escape the city during the trial scene."

"I am with you. I brought all that I need with me. We can leave together." Alexia's tears dried upon her cheeks.

Yeshua explained, "We will wait here until the performances begin. The soldiers will be expecting me to be in the performance at the east end of the Roman road. Once they see that I am not there, they will come looking for me here."

Yeshua paced from one end of his hut to the other. He picked up various items from the floor as he hurried to prepare for their departure. He walked to the window to look out across the compound. It was still early. No one had begun to move around the grounds.

"But first, I must go say goodbye to my parents," Yeshua announced while looking out of the window. Alexia was not sure if he was talking to her or himself.

"You must do what you must. Please be careful. We don't know if the soldiers are watching your parents or not," Alexia said. "Do not worry about me. My escorts will remain outside and keep watch."

Yeshua responded, "I will be careful. It should only take me a few moments. If I am not back by the time the sun is up, meet me at the foothills of the mountains."

Alexia was taken aback by the simplicity of Yeshua's instructions. He was usually quite detailed when it came to giving instructions.

"Do not wait for me here any longer than is necessary," he explained.

"Yason, your words are frightening me," Alexia began to cry again. "Please promise me you will not be too long. Or perhaps, I should come with you." Alexia gathered her belongings to show that going with Yeshua was the only option.

"No, you must stay here," Yeshua said, raising his voice. "We cannot draw attention to ourselves by being seen together."

Alexia immediately stopped in her tracks and withdrew her position from the entrance.

"I promise to be back soon. Nothing will keep me from being with you," Yeshua said to her. "Not even Roman soldiers. Besides, I need your help with packing a few more things. We can go when I return."

Yeshua used the east exit to avoid being seen by Alexia's guardians. No one could detect his movements from the east side of the hut. He quickly moved toward the backside of the compound to keep from awakening any of the pigs. Yeshua walked on the narrow grassy area adjacent to the gravel along the path leading toward his parents' house. Although it was his usual route, this time, he took extra caution.

The sound of footsteps seemed to be louder during the early morning. There was no apparent reason for this. Perhaps the thin cold air allowed sounds to echo more during this time. The reality of what was about to happen started to engross Yeshua. He walked carefully and felt like a prisoner in his home. His performances' famous character would never again allow Yeshua to have the anonymity he had previously enjoyed.

As Yeshua got closer to his parent's compound, he was startled by the sound of unusual voices emanating from the house. They were the voices of strangers whom he did not recognize. So, instead of moving toward the front entrance, he quickly ran to the back and listened through the side window.

"It is imperative that we find your son today. You must have some idea where we can find him," one of the voices said calmly and matter-of-factly. The voice was heavy, deep, obviously Greek, and male. The voice came from someone of official authority.

"We have not seen our son for days now. He is angry with me because I did not support his performances against the emperor," Samuel attempted to persuade the soldiers.

"It is true," Miriam added. "He is a stubborn man with ideas of his own. We have tried to teach him better, but he listens to no one."

"Simon the governor wants him taken into custody today. We have our orders. As you can see, they are sealed by the emperor," the soldier said as he took out the scroll of parchment. He showed it to Samuel and Miriam.

They both looked intently at the warrant. Neither of them could read the inscription, but they did not want the soldier to know it.

"So, if you know anything about his whereabouts, I advise you to tell us at once. If the emperor finds out you are hiding him, there will be a price to pay," the soldier sternly warned them.

Samuel and Miriam showed no obvious reaction on their faces to the soldier's threat. They simply stood quietly by the door as the soldier proceeded to leave. Miriam immediately thought she should run to Yeshua's hut and warn him about the soldiers. Even before the soldier could leave, her imagination was already detailing the way she would tell Yeshua the news. In her mind, Yeshua will more likely heed the warning if it was coming from his mother.

After the soldiers left, Yeshua did not hesitate to rush toward the entrance of his parents' home. He usually waited at the front door to be given Samuel's permission to enter, but there was no time to do what was customary.

WAITING TO EXIT

Meanwhile, Alexia waited for Yeshua to return. She nervously paced the floor. Multiple possible scenarios raced through her mind about how life would change for them. The journey to the next village was a long and hard one by foot. Alexia had only traveled the path toward Yeriho once while riding in a cart pulled by horses. The fables and tales about the road always spoke about the dangers for unsuspecting travelers.

One of the most famous stories had to do with a man who was robbed and left for dead.[1] He lay in a ravine off the west side of the road. Alexia remembered the story from childhood. Because of her father's position in Rome, she was taught by tutors at home. These tutors often had biased opinions about Judean traditions but wanted to be respectful of young girls' religious education.

Alexia recalled that the man in the story lay dying in the ravine as both a priest and Levite passed by him. Both saw the man in his desperate condition and chose to pass by on the far side of the road. Some said they were in a hurry to get to the temple and synagogue to carry out their responsibilities. Others said they thought the man was dead and wanted to honor the laws that declared those unclean for touching a dead body. It seemed everyone had a spin on the story.

Then a man of Ethiopian origin came by and saw the man lying in the ravine. He hesitated at first to come to the man's aide. He feared that the robbers might be nearby. Or even worse, that the man may have been one of the robbers and was faking so that he could draw in an unsuspecting victim. Despite his fears and concerns, the Ethiopian decided to crawl down the ravine to the man to see if he was still alive and if he could help him. As he

---

1. Luke 10:25–37.

drew closer to the man, he saw the man's severe injuries. Fresh blood spilled from his side to the ground, and the smell of sweat and decay was in the air around him.

After examining the man's wounds, the Ethiopian carried him on his back up the ravine to the road where his mule was resting. He then hoisted the man up onto the mule sideways, arms hanging over one side, legs over the other. He dangled back and forth as the mule walked up the Yeriho road. Once in town, the Ethiopian found a hostel and paid for three nights' lodging. He promised to return after the three days to check on the man. He also paid for one of the women to change and dress the man's bandages each day. The Ethiopian never asked about the identity of the man. Some people who told the story said that the man was of North African origin. Others claimed he was of Asia Minor descent.

Reflecting on the story of the Ethiopian solicited many fears about traveling with Yeshua to Yeriho. Yeshua's father had a friend who could offer refuge once they arrived in the city. Traveling at night on foot would take several days. Because of the oppressive heat of the daytime, most of the journey typically took place at night. The longer she waited for Yeshua, the more intense her anxiety about the trip increased.

He is taking longer than I expected, she thought as the time became protracted. *I hope he is not in any danger.*

Her imagination wandered from the Ethiopian story and returned to contemplating the possibility that Yeshua and his entire family were taken into custody. Waiting with nothing to do made Alexia's feelings of helplessness even more inescapable. First, she thought about returning to her father's palace in case news about Yeshua's possible arrest had been reported. She did not want Yeshua to return while she was away and leave without her. The dilemma produced overwhelming feelings. She felt torn between her love for Yeshua and her loyalty to her family.

"How is this happening?" Alexia asked herself. "Who am I, and why am I here?"

Chapter 10

The Way

THE SUDDEN SOUND OF footsteps on the gravel path leading to Yeshua's home caused a surge of relief to flood Alexia's body. Her heart leaped with excitement. She raced quickly toward the entrance on the east side of the hut. It was the common entrance for Yeshua and anyone familiar with his home, built of stone and encased in the side of the hills on the west side.

Her feelings of elation were immediately eclipsed by the appearance of a statuesque figure standing at the entrance. It was Lucifer standing in her full military adornments with a sinister smile on her face, blocking any chance of Alexia's escape. The escorts were seen lying on the ground outside the entrance, dead or simply knocked unconscious, Lucifer and her soldiers being the likely culprits.

"I was not expecting to see you here," Lucifer said as she glanced around the room. She took careful note of the lounge arrangement and fire pit in the middle of the room. It was a sign that a meeting took place for more than just a few people.

"Does your father know you are here in these parts?" Lucifer inquired. "I have heard the rumors about you two. So, I guess it must be so."

Lucifer also noticed the packed bag sitting on the ground by Alexia.

"Are we planning a trip somewhere?" she asked.

Alexia remained silent for the moment as she attempted to construct a plausible explanation of her presence at Yeshua's home. Lucifer did not wait for Alexia to explain her presence or Yeshua's whereabouts.

"How would your father feel about your involvement in this situation?" she continued to interrogate Alexia.

Lucifer, also surprised by this new turn of events, paced the floor as she thought about ways to capitalize on the current discovery. "I am sure you have not told your father about this. Because if he had the slightest inclination that you were helping Yeshua, he would have told me and given me exclusive permission to deal with you myself," Lucifer said with confidence. She paused before continuing her rant while also thinking about the entrapment possibilities. "So, since your father doesn't know about your involvement, this presents many other opportunities for you and me."

Finally, Alexia broke her silence now that she had a better understanding of what Lucifer might have in mind. "Opportunities like what?" she asked Lucifer. She had no intention of cooperating with Lucifer, yet Alexia chose to be inquisitive.

Lucifer smiled, "Well, since you asked. As one woman to another and one Roman to another, it all depends on what you are willing to do to protect your man."

"I don't know what you are talking about," Alexia said.

She knew just what Lucifer meant. Putting herself at risk of being charged with treason for the sake of Yeshua's cause proved how deeply she was in love with him. She was willing to do almost anything for him. Every woman knows this truth. It is the truth that runs through all the ancient Judean parables. Eve, Sarah, Esther, Rachel, the list goes on and on. Women who love at the expense of their safety and well-being.

"You know what I am talking about," Lucifer raised her voice above the previous mellow tone. "You don't have to explain it or confess it to me. Just your mere presence here tells me all that I need to know. So, woman to woman, I propose to you that we both have interests in this situation. I am sure there is some reasonable agreement we can make that will ensure that your dirty little secret is not discovered, and I can get what I am looking for." Lucifer paused again to give Alexia time to ponder what was just said to her. "I need to bring Yeshua back with me to the emperor's palace. If you help me do this, I can assure you that your secret stays safe. You can return home to your father, and everything will be as it was before."

Lucifer stood some twelve or more inches taller than Alexia. She pranced over to where Alexia was standing, stood behind her, and leaned in close to her left ear. She whispered, "You will go home, and we will act like none of this ever happened. You and I both know that you are no street peasant. You cannot survive out here in the wilderness. Like the prophet said, 'No one can live by bread alone.'"

Alexia was astonished by the offer made by Lucifer and decided to speak up. "Get from behind me, Lucifer!" She turned around, facing Lucifer and looking up at her much taller challenger, and shouted in anger, "You, of all people, should be aware of my father's friendship with Simon, the governor of this province. I will have you arrested for making such threats against a friend of the royal family. What makes you think I am here as an ally of Yeshua and not an investigator?" she stated with conviction.

Alexia's response was smart and not anticipated by Lucifer. Lucifer appeared to be taken aback by the response and the intensity of Alexia's demeanor. Lucifer was not accustomed to encountering females that demonstrated an equal assertiveness.

Lucifer sensed the need to retreat from her inquiry. She said, "I am quite aware of who you were and meant no threat against you. I was simply offering protection from what appeared to be a compromising situation. Forgive me if I came across as inappropriate in any way." Lucifer's voice changed to a more conciliatory tone.

"Your actions are understandable given the appearances," Alexia said. "But things are not always what they appear to be. For example, it has appeared to many in the palace that you have a special relationship with the emperor. Of course, between us two women, we know that is not true. People talk about what they do not know and what they do not know they simply make it up. Do you know what I mean?"

Lucifer, who prided herself as being the master of inquisition and trickery, realized that Alexia had outwitted her. So, she quickly announced her exit.

"I see exactly what you mean. I will now make my way back to the palace and allow you to continue your investigation," Lucifer said as she prepared her departure.

As Lucifer motioned toward the east exit of the hut, Alexia reached for the fold of her right arm and looked her in the eyes. "Thank you, Lucifer. I think for both of our sakes that the knowledge of this meeting should stay between us?"

"I agree, and I pledge to keep this between us. Woman to woman." Lucifer smiled, left the room quickly, and exited into the night.

Alexia breathed a sigh of relief as Lucifer disappeared out of sight. Her mind also relaxed from the exhaustion of the rapid flow of alternative thoughts and ideas plaguing her brain. She now shifted her focus again to the most important thing on her mind.

"Where is Yason?" she asked herself, not aware of the passage of time.

Since she was inside and unable to observe the sky, it was impossible to know how long it had been since Yeshua had left to see his parents. Feelings of relief over Lucifer's confrontation were soon to be overshadowed by the anxiety of wondering what happened to Yeshua. Since Lucifer made no mention of having captured Yeshua, Alexia assumed he must be still with his parents. Leaving to search for him was not a prudent option. Other possibilities of Yeshua's whereabouts began to make their entry into her consciousness.

Maybe he never made it to his parents, Alexia thought. *Perhaps on his way to see them, he decided it might be best for him to run away without me or to say good-bye to his parents?* This thought was the most dreadful of the possibilities.

Suddenly Alexia's heart began to sink deep inside her stomach. A throbbing pain of grief began to pound against her insides. Overwhelmed with emotions, she fell to the ground and wept. Amid her sobs, Alexia could suddenly hear footsteps. In the distant night, the familiar sound of Yeshua stepping on the soft gravel outside his hut brought immediate consolation to her fears. Slightly hesitant, Alexia raised her head and looked toward the east entrance as Yeshua entered the room. Emotions consumed her thoughts as she rediscovered the passions that first led to their love.

Yeshua's tall frame, dark complexion, and long curly hair rolled in locks made his appearance resemble a Nazarite priest of old—except with a flair of style and elegance. His long legs moved his entire body with so much grace. It reminded Alexia of the giraffes imported from the African deserts being unloaded at the coastal markets. His physical presence infused the entire room with feelings of comfort and security.

Alexia always felt secure whenever Yeshua was around. His affection was a blanket of emotional comfort for her. Especially under the current circumstances, seeing Yeshua safe and sound excited within Alexia the re-newed courage she needed to claim her emancipation.

The first thing Yeshua noticed upon entering the room was the fear and concern on Alexia's face. Rescuing her from anything that threatened her happiness was an instinctual response for him. Just the image of her sitting on the floor with fear in her beautiful brown eyes ignited in him the need to come to her aide, to take her away from all the pain and struggle, and to see once again the smile on her face.

"That's your problem, Yeshua," he could still hear his mother's voice. "You are so giving and generous to these young women. They always take advantage of men like you."

Alexia was not like the other women. None of them would have been willing to give up so much to be with him. This simple truth was more than enough for Yeshua to forget all that his mother warned him about and to surrender his heart to life on the run with Alexia.

Knowing this about Alexia made Yeshua unafraid of anything or anyone. He was not afraid of the emperor, Lucifer, his parents, or what the people would say about him when he was gone. All that mattered was that Alexia was still there waiting for him. She did not choose to leave and return to the peace and luxury of her father's home as he had feared. Now they could be together forever in a place where they did not have to worry about what other people thought or deal with their relationship's social and political ramifications.

Suddenly, Alexia could hear groans of pain coming from her two escorts, who were still lying unconscious on the ground. Although she was relieved to know they were alive, their movement made it even more urgent for Yeshua and her to make their escape. Once fully awake, they would assume she was captured by Lucifer and return to report it to her father. By then, they would be well on their way.

LUCIFER FACES THADDEUS

Lucifer returned to the emperor's palace in her chariot while accompanied by her assigned regiment of soldiers. She was still perplexed by her encounter with Alexia. She pondered just how to explain to the emperor about her failure to capture Yeshua. The evening was getting late as the moon appeared high in the northern sky. Nights during early spring were often cool. The clouds had cleared like curtains, allowing the stars to shine brightly as the backdrop to the luminous moon.

None of these atmospheric phenomena were on Lucifer's mind as she entered the emperor's quarters' front gates. By the time she arrived, the emperor was in his study reading the reports from the various investigators who patrolled the villages' streets. The soldiers who accompanied Lucifer to Yeshua's village had already returned and filed their report. There was no way to anticipate the emperor's reaction to the news that Yeshua had evaded capture and the street performances were to occur as planned.

Lucifer stood in the doorway of Thaddeus's study. She intentionally wore garments that accentuated her long and slender frame, and her breasts stood upright behind the leather breastplate of her uniform. She was not taking any chances with the emperor's disappointment at the reports of the day.

"My lord. May I enter your chamber with my report?" Lucifer waited patiently for Thaddeus to finish reading the scrolls containing the soldiers' reports.

Finally, Thaddeus looked toward the doorway and waved Lucifer toward him with his right hand, "Yes, you may enter."

Thaddeus immediately noticed Lucifer's sensuous attire and the accents of her body behind the tight-fitting uniform. He desired to have his way with her, but he felt compelled to keep their conversation formal for the moment.

"The written reports of today are a bit disappointing," Thaddeus spoke while he pretended to read. He hoped his face would not indicate the fantasies in his mind. However, it was too late. Lucifer had already noticed the way his eyes moved up and down her body when she first entered the room. "So then, what is your next move?" he asked.

Lucifer felt some relief at the question. It seemed to give her an alternative to the planned excuse for not having captured Yeshua. She must not allow too much time to pass before giving Thaddeus an answer. Her response needed to show confidence and control of the situation and not indicate that Yeshua evaded capture.

"I spoke with the daughter of a prominent Roman citizen tonight who is conspiring with Simon the governor. She is prepared to assist us in our plans," Lucifer said. She hoped the explanation was convincing since the emperor and the governor seldom had direct communication with each other.

"That is good to know. What is she willing to do to help? I will settle for nothing less than Yeshua in my custody and his silly performances canceled," the emperor responded.

Thaddeus still spoke in the official tone of his role as emperor. He was careful not to make the usual exceptions that he did for Lucifer. Lucifer waited before answering, not because she was concerned about the fabricated story she just presented to him, but because of the unexpected sensation that she felt inside her pelvic area. She forgot the effect assertive and confident men had on her. The sheer sound of Thaddeus's voice caused her respirations to increase as each breath rose in her chest, visible even behind her uniform's breastplate. The emperor's sudden motion of his eyes down toward her chest confirmed his awareness of her excitement.

"She has agreed to cooperate fully with me as a witness in the investigation. We will capture Yeshua by dawn and have him here by noon."

"This is good to know. I trust you will deliver him to me by noon. It is getting late. I must retire for the evening. But perhaps before you leave, we can share in a drink of wine."

The gesture was risky. Petula had already gone to bed for the evening. The emperor usually reserved the stone recliners in the room for special gatherings of four or more men. The recliners formed a U-shape, with soft pillows at each station, designed so that each man could recline by leaning to his left while holding his goblet in his right hand. Thaddeus pointed

Lucifer in the direction of the room and she readily followed him. With every step toward the recliner, Lucifer could feel the moisture accumulating between her legs.

"A fresh supply of wine was delivered just this evening," Thaddeus announced as he walked behind Lucifer into his lounge.

He gently touched his hand on the small of her back. Lucifer suddenly stopped as if to appear startled, but soon made it clear that the move was intentional. She returned the courtesy by pressing her backside firmly against his body. After a while, they both were committed to the wine and the full disclosure of the energy generated between them. It had been months since they had been together. As they reclined on the stone couch, the passion exploded between them as they surrendered to each other.

After they finished their lovemaking, Lucifer quickly rose and began to put on her uniform. Thaddeus, who remained unclothed on the couch, reached for her hand.

"Why are you in a hurry?" he asked.

"Remember, my lord, I have work to do," Lucifer replied. She wanted to avoid Thaddeus opening the door for a more detailed questioning about her plans.

"I remember, but your beauty makes it hard to let you leave. Sit here and stay for a little longer," Thaddeus motioned for Lucifer to sit down on his bare lap. Lucifer was still standing with her garter belt in hand. Thaddeus reached and pulled the belt from her.

ON THE RUN

"We must hurry if we are going to make it in time before my guardians awake," Alexia shouted to Yeshua as he finished packing the last of his most valuable items.

Knowing the length and risk of the journey, Yeshua was selective about what he wanted to take with him. While he packed, it occurred to him that this would be the first time in his life he would be away from the farm without his father. They often traveled together to deliver meat to markets in neighboring villages. It took several days, so they spent some nights with one of his uncles.

Trips with his father and brothers were the happiest times they shared. He had never given much thought to it before now. His mother's presence sometimes created tension in their family that was not there whenever the men were together without her. Maybe they all tried too hard to please her. Perhaps they competed against each other for the position as the first man of the home. As he folded each piece of clothing, thoughts about his parents flooded his mind. There would be so many unanswered questions. Why did he need to run away? Was it their fault? What could they have done to prevent him from running away?

Yeshua intentionally selected items that carried special meaning and memories. These included fire sticks, leftover bread from the last meal his mother prepared, and a braided bracelet his father gave him when he turned sixteen. The bracelet came from the hide of what turned out to be one of his father's most profitable pigs.

The last item was the most difficult one to pack. It was a medium-sized sword used to cut the tails off the young pigs. Yeshua was responsible for this task most of his life. He usually cut the tails after the piglets were two weeks old. Yeshua never got used to the squealing sounds made when he clipped their tails.

"Do we need that?" Alexia asked when she saw Yeshua glide his hand above the top of the sword's blade. He was careful about always keeping the edge sharpened and ready for use.

"You can never know," Yeshua said without taking his eyes off the tip of the blade. "I hope we don't have to use it, but I am not going to take any chances."

Yeshua was adamant about the need for protection, leaving no room for discussion. Alexia did not offer any protest. She was well aware of the danger and the possibilities of what could happen to them if caught together. Yeshua placed the sword in the side sleeve of the bag. Only the dark wooden handle could be seen, stained with blood and sweat sealed between the fine cedar wood grains.

Yeshua kept his focus on the task at hand with very little awareness of the anxiety building in his body. The reality of leaving his mother and father almost overwhelmed him. He thought, *It is good that Alexia is here with me. Otherwise, I would probably change my mind and stay home. She needs me to be strong.*

THROUGH THE VALLEY OF DEATH

Moving through the small village at night came with its own set of challenges. Fortunately, Yeshua grew up on a farm and knew how to navigate his way through the maze of pig pens and pastures. To successfully make it to the Yeriho road, Alexia would have to trust Yeshua in ways she had never trusted another man.

The biggest challenge had to do with timing. Although the evening was late, and most people were asleep; some animals were more nocturnal than others. It only took the barking of one suspecting dog to arouse the curiosity of the other animals. Most of the dogs were nonhostile and knew Yeshua's smell. But occasionally, a barking dog indicated a friendly response to a familiar scent. Yeshua was careful to take the eastern route around the pig pens located furthest away from the main houses. The lessons learned as a young boy from the many times of sneaking away from home at night prepared him to navigate toward the village's perimeter safely.

Alexia was also keenly aware of the sights and sounds around the village from her many excursions to see Yeshua. She would make surreptitious visits in the middle of the day when the farm was most active, and people were distracted by their work assignments. Taking the journey in the evening provided a new perspective about life on the farm and how privileged life had been for her. Most of her exposure came from observing servants who harvested the crops on her father's land. The gusts of wind in the valley inlets that separated the mountains from the village stirred a malodor in the air. Alexia wondered why Yeshua was taking a route that presented various obstacles.

"Yason, are you sure we are going the best way?" Alexia finally asked.

"Yes, I have been this way several times. It is the only way that allows us not to be seen or heard by the workers," Yeshua explained.

"I trust that you know the way. I will follow your lead," Alexia reassured him.

As they came to the edge of the farm that rested against the valley floor, Yeshua hesitated. They reached the darkest side of the farm where the mountain range eclipsed the moon's light. It had the advantage of providing a cover for their escape. However, it prevented a clear vision of what was ahead of them.

In the distance, Yeshua could hear water flowing down the side of the hill, emptying into a small stream that led toward the back of the farm. It was a major water supply for the pigs during the dawn feeding. Yeshua could hear the water, but he could not see where the stream ended. He wanted to be careful that they did not fall into the stream against the rocks and possibly injure themselves.

"What is that up ahead?" pointed Alexia. "I saw someone move." Immediately, Yeshua's heart began to beat faster as his eyes pierced through the darkness to focus on the tall shadowy figure coming towards them.

"Stay behind me." Yeshua pressed Alexia's body behind him. He had no other recourse given their proximity away from the farm with no other objects to hide behind.

As the figure slowly moved toward them, the image of a man riding a horse began to develop. Still relatively hidden by the night's darkness, the rider's movement on a horse did not seem to pose any immediate danger. Roman soldiers never travel alone. They were always in groups of ten to one hundred. The lone mysterious figure slowly dismounted the horse as he came closer. Yeshua briefly thought about lighting his torch but decided not to make any sudden moves. As it stood, neither party could see each other.

"Stay behind me, Alexia. Don't make a move until I say so," Yeshua ordered as he felt her body squirming against his back.

Once the tall figure was within a few meters, Yeshua made the first move, "Who goes there?" The figure did not answer. Yeshua quickly reached in his bag, hanging over his left shoulder, and placed his hand on the handle of the sword. His heart raced faster as his breathing became more labored. Sweat began dripping from his face into his beard.

"Who are you, and what do you want?" Yeshua asked one more time, hoping to appear unafraid of the stranger in the night.

"So, are we going somewhere tonight?" The voice was all too familiar to Alexia. Yeshua had never had direct contact with Lucifer.

Lucifer had a distinct sound to her voice. It was unique to her and different from anyone else in the entire province. The tone was more authoritarian than most women and echoed through the air on the open plains. It was not only the sound, but the way in which Lucifer spoke that gave her voice its signature quality.

"I knew I would find you two here. I just had to be patient and wait." Lucifer smiled as she delighted in the terror seen on Alexia's face.

Her decision to leave the emperor on the couch, even after he begged her to stay, proved to be a wise decision. It was a choice not many women would have been able to make once they were in the clutches of Thaddeus's arms.

"Did you come after me alone?" asked Yeshua.

"No, I have a nice cohort of soldiers waiting over the hill there. All I have to do is light my torch and raise it to give the signal, and you both will be taken into my custody," Lucifer boasted.

Lucifer's gaze at Alexia communicated that she was giving her a chance to be spared further embarrassment. Her father would be humiliated to know that his daughter had colluded with a Judean revolutionary. But Alexia stood firmly next to Yeshua.

"I am where I need to be," she said.

Meanwhile, Yeshua firmly gripped the knife's handle in his side bag, cloaked from Lucifer's view. The cover of the night made it impossible to see what the other person was doing or about to do.

"What do you want with me, Lucifer?" Yeshua inquired. "I am of no concern to you. We are leaving town, so I will no longer be a threat to you or the emperor."

Yeshua hoped his line of reasoning would convince Lucifer to allow them to escape. His absence would mean the end of the street performances and their effects on the minds of the people. Unfortunately, merely resolving the threat was not the real motive. She longed for only two things—power and control. Likewise, for the emperor, it was not enough for Yeshua to just disappear. There needed to be a public demonstration before the people to prove once and for all that Thaddeus was the absolute supreme ruler. Yeshua being paraded around the streets while being scourged with a whip would show what happens to those who disregard the authority of the Roman government—this would be the only adequate final performance.

"It will not be that easy for you," said Lucifer to Yeshua. "You have dishonored your name and your father's name. You have offended Emperor Thaddeus, the son of the gods and ruler of the world. Your dramas make a mockery of his power and name. You have misled the people with your foolish fables and distorted ideas about this mythical character you call Jesus. For this, you will be held accountable. It is my charge to bring you back to the emperor alive to face your sentencing in his courts.

"And you, Alexia, have brought dishonor to the doorsteps of your father," Lucifer said. "You are no longer considered his daughter and must suffer accordingly. So, prepare yourselves to be taken into my custody."

Lucifer walked closer to Yeshua, towering above him and looking down into his face with disgust, as Alexia remained hidden behind him. She then moved slowly toward Alexia and stood beside her. This allowed the soldiers who were waiting in the distance to be in their line of sight.

Yeshua, no longer waiting to see if Lucifer would allow them to leave freely, pulled his hand out of the side bag. As Lucifer maneuvered around him, toward his left shoulder, Yeshua reached for the handle of the sword in his bag. In a rapid, back-handed motion, he thrust the sword in Lucifer's chest just beneath her right breast. Lucifer bellowed in pain.

Because of the darkness, it was not at first apparent the source of the pain. Lucifer did not anticipate Yeshua's swift and daring action. It soon became clear what had happened to her and who did it. The tip of the blade penetrated the protective armor of her breastplate, causing both intense pain and excitement. But the mixture of the two sensations was only temporary because the pain overcame the excitement. Lucifer birthed more screams into the night as her body staggered helplessly to the ground beneath.

The sound of Lucifer's cries could be heard for miles. The surrounding mountain range provided the natural acoustics needed for her screams to be heard by the soldiers. Lucifer's horse recognized the sound first. Her threatening shudder alarmed the other horses, causing the soldiers to react simultaneously. The captain of the squad could see that the tallest of the dark figures as it fell like a tree in the forest. He surmised that something was wrong and activated the other soldiers.

Although he did not know the circumstances, the lead soldier was fully aware of the consequences of not acting if Lucifer needed him.

"Charge forward to the target," yelled the captain.

Instantly, each soldier mounted their horses and rushed into the night. The captain led the way with his torch held high in the air. The thunderous sound of the horses' hooves shattered the silence and signaled an immediate response by Yeshua and Alexia.

Yeshua knew that the soldiers would arrive without delay. He reached for Alexia's hand to alert her to the urgency of the moment and used his free hand to withdraw the sword from the chest of Lucifer. He entertained the notion of pressing his sword further into the chest cavity, or better yet, taking it out and thrusting it again closer to her heart.

A sobering thought invaded his mind, "I am a street performer, not a murderer." Nevertheless, the immediate need was to escape and run away. So, he pulled Alexia close to his side as they began to run toward the wooded path.

As Alexia and Yeshua ran toward the Yeriho road, the soldiers reached Lucifer's body. She was lying on the ground with blood draining from the wound in her chest. The captain was the first to reach her and asked if he could help. Lucifer was consumed by the idea that a peasant street performer had undone her. She also considered the repercussions if the emperor knew this. So, she ordered the captain to proceed with their pursuit of the fugitives.

"But my lord, you are bleeding," the captain expressed concern in case his loyalties came into question later.

Lucifer clutched the captain by the inside of his left elbow and pulled him closer to her. By then, too much blood was lost, and she could barely speak, but the look in her eyes conveyed to the captain the desperation of having to capture Yeshua. It was something worth more than her life or the lives of any of the soldiers.

As life slowly slipped from Lucifer, a decision whether to pursue Yeshua and Alexia needed to be made. On the one hand, Lucifer needed to be carried back to the palace to receive immediate medical treatment. On the other hand, Yeshua and Alexia were hastily making their way toward the Yeriho path, which was just a few kilometers away. They could disappear in the night and easily find refuge in one of the barrows of the forest.

The captain ordered five of his men to carry Lucifer to the wagon reserved for Yeshua and Alexia. Two Arabian-bred horses were hitched and ready for quick retrieval.

"Bring the wagon over here. Two of you will ride next to Lucifer, keeping constant pressure on the wounds during the ride," yelled the captain.

Experience had taught him first-aid skills on the battlefield. He learned the importance of securing a wound while riding in a vehicle driven by well-trained horses as the wheels bounced over dry, dusty fields, dodging the multiple holes and rocks. Two soldiers rode up front. One steered while the other held up a torched lantern to both see the roadway and to watch for possible signs of ambush.

"They may not be working alone on their escape," the captain ordered. He was direct and clear, very much aware of the high stakes, as Lucifer slowly slipped into unconsciousness.

"Hurry!" he screamed.

It was time to refocus the captain's attention on the escape of Yeshua and Alexia. They were still in his sight but slowly transforming into dark ghostly figures against the backdrop of the soft moonlight. He assumed the female was slowing their escape, and that would give him and the soldiers ample time to catch up with them. The captain and the remaining two soldiers hurried on foot toward the entrance of the Yeriho passageway.

"Come, let us pursue them," the captain motioned to the two accompanying soldiers.

They immediately followed behind the captain. They ran in the same cadence of well-trained soldiers, covering one meter of ground per second. The captain, slightly older than the twenty-year-old soldiers, excelled physically above them both. He pushed them to their limits as they ran toward their targets. The gap quickly began to close between them.

The captain explained in detail how they would apprehend the fugitives as they ran at full pace. The two younger soldiers were mesmerized by the captain's pulmonary fitness. Their leader spoke unhindered without taking full breaths into his lungs between each sentence.

"Prepare to flank them as we get closer. I will give you the signal. One of you will flank to my left, the other to my right. I will charge forward up the middle directly toward them," the captain explained.

"Hurry, Yason. The soldiers are coming," Alexia called out as they ran toward the forest alongside the road.

Yeshua, although taller than Alexia, was no comparison to her speed and agility. Alexia often competed in foot races sponsored by the emperor.

The sound of the soldiers running toward them was getting louder with each passing moment. As they reached the path's descent into the forest, they could hear the soldiers running along the ridge high above them. They ran hard and carefully, doing their best not to get caught in the brush and thickets that marked the pathway adjacent to the forest.

"We must make it into the forest," Alexia ordered.

Being the daughter of a wealthy slave owner, Alexia was accustomed to giving orders and directions to others. Yeshua was the youngest son in his family and was accustomed to receiving orders. Therefore, it felt natural for him to follow directions.

"We must pick up our pace. As soon as we enter the forest, let's go to the right. We need to find a place to crawl into that will conceal us," she said.

Upon entering the forest, Alexia and Yeshua quickly found a place to hide in the dense brush underneath one of the cedar trees. The force from numerous windstorms had formed a natural arch between two trees, creating what appeared to be a cave. In the darkness, even with lit torches, it was unlikely the soldiers would find them.

"We may need to spend the night here and leave during the early dawn—before the sun rises," Yeshua suggested.

They could now hear the soldiers debating among themselves about who should enter the forest first. They sounded unsure and worried about what might be ahead of them. None of them wanted to suffer the same fate as Lucifer. If they were not panic-stricken, it would have been comical to hear Roman soldiers seem bewildered and afraid. Ironically, combat soldiers were known for their acts of bravery. Yeshua and Alexia held silent with the hope that they would eventually abandon their pursuit, even if that meant telling a lie to the emperor about why they were unable to capture them.

"Both of you enter one at a time," commanded the captain.

He was accustomed to sending men into places that he did not want to go. The two soldiers looked at each other. One seemed to know what the other was thinking, but neither of them said anything. One of them was thinking about the possibility of murdering the captain and leaving him at the edge of the forest. He reasoned that there would be no witnesses to tell what happened. It was not that the soldiers were afraid to die. Yet, neither of them wanted to lose his life chasing a meaningless peasant whose only crime was street performing. There were better causes to die for.

"Sir, is this worth the risk of dying? Should we return and say they got away from us? We can blame it all on having to care for Lucifer," the soldier suggested. The captain seemed convinced by the plan. He looked at each soldier to confirm their mutual understanding. Both nodded in agreement.

"I think they are going to go back?" Alexia whispered.

It became apparent to her that the soldiers were not going to take the risk of crossing the border into the forest. She began to relax but remained cautious. Yeshua let out a sigh of relief and sat down on the ground just under one of the trees. He needed time to allow his mind to catch up with his body's exasperation from all the events that just happened.

"I love you, Yason. I want you to know that is the only reason why I am here. Not for fame or fortune. I love you enough to be here with you no matter what the cost," Alexia declared as she tried to slow her breathing.

"Thank you, Alexia," Yeshua responded. "You mean the world to me. I have given it all away to be here with you." The words appeared to come from one of the scenes in his dramas. The dreadful feelings and sounds of being pursued by Roman soldiers suddenly faded into the night air. "You are the most remarkable person I have ever known in my life. I pledge my love and my life to you. Your people would be my people, your enemies shall be my enemies, and your God will be my God."

"Yason, you are a wonderful man," Alexia repaid the tribute. "My life has been transformed by being with you. Being with you is more than I could have ever imagined. I commit myself to you and all that you believe in and fight for. I promise never to leave you or forsake you. Whatever you need from me, I will offer. You will never be alone."

The conversation between Alexia and Yeshua began to take on marital overtones. Amid the danger awaiting them on the Yeriho road, the love between them produced feelings of safety and refuge. When it became clear that the soldiers had left, Yeshua took his right arm and extended it around Alexia's upper back slightly below her breasts. Yeshua caressed Alexia's upper back and then eased his hand to her side to massage the area near her breasts. Alexia instantly responded to Yeshua's touch.

The evening had fully settled, and there was no need to make any attempts to travel any further. The day was coming to an end and tomorrow waited with new adventures and challenges. They made their bed on the soft ground just inside the protective folds of the forest.

Yeshua took off his cloak and spread it neatly over the ground beneath them. Alexia took her wrap from her head, allowing her hair to fall below her shoulders freely. She created a soft headrest for Yeshua as he lay on his back.

Then she opened her stole to reveal each breast to the evening air, which caused an immediate reaction that ran deep inside her. Yeshua sensed the moment and responded on point, as they both agreed that tonight had to be special because it might be their last.

Chapter 11

Death

THE RIDE BACK TO the palace was brutal. Like those in the infamous chariot races at the emperor's stadium, the soldiers drove the horses at phenomenal speeds. The movement over the rugged roads caused the cart to shake fiercely in the night. The decision was made not to attempt the journey to Rome but to go to the governor's palace in Galilee. The travel to Galilee lasted well into the night.

Lucifer fell in and out of consciousness several times along the journey. She often hallucinated and swore to the gods. It was impossible for the soldier tasked with applying pressure to the wound to keep his hand in place under the conditions. Everyone, especially Lucifer, knew that the attempt to make it back to the governor in time for medical attention was futile.

As the moments passed by, Lucifer stared at the sky and beheld the radiance of the full moon. Breathing became increasingly painful as she could sense the life flowing slowly from her body. Everyone's mind in the chariot focused on the same person. Not the person dying, but on Thaddeus, the emperor.

Even in her catatonic state, Lucifer imagined how Thaddeus would take the news of her death. It would take several days before knowledge of her demise reached Rome. She entertained memories of the two of them and their first meeting. He was the youngest emperor in the history of Rome. Being several years older than Thaddeus, Lucifer was impressed at his youthful maturity and intellectual prowess. He introduced himself to her at the front courtyard of the palace at the inaugural celebration. His face was so innocent. Her chariot was to be his escort to the stadium.

At the time, her primary responsibility was security, ensuring that all palace residents were safe from any unexpected terrorist acts. The Zealots were particularly active at the time, and many worried they had infiltrated the ranks of the palace guards.

Suddenly, Lucifer's reminiscing was interrupted when the cart hit a large hole. Lucifer screamed in pain, "Damn you all!" The rural roads were nothing in comparison to the paved ones in the city. *It is amazing the thoughts that enter the mind when you are dying.*

The soldiers looked up at each other as the cart bounced in the air and came crashing back to earth. They too, were preoccupied with thoughts of the emperor.

What if she dies in our custody? Will the governor think we killed her?

No one dared to say anything aloud. Lucifer might be dying, but the fear people had of her was still very much alive. The soldiers saw it as their duty to make the journey as quickly as possible. They knew it might mean their deaths in the end.

After a few hours, Lucifer slipped into the final coma. Her breathing became shallow as her complexion turned pale and ashy. A blue tint started to settle around the corners of her lips. The soldier that had applied pressure to her wound slowly removed his hand from her dead body, which no longer resisted the cart's erratic movements. The muscles in her face retreated as her body relaxed. It swayed freely with the stride of the horses.

"Slow the horses," yelled the soldier who was next to the dead body.

The driver sensed something had changed and immediately called the horses to attention. Instinctually, the horses felt the presence of death in the air and offered no resistance to the driver's command. Slowly the cart came to a dead stop. The soldiers said nothing at first. They just looked at one another.

Finally, the driver asked, "Is she dead?"

The others simply nodded.

"We are all dead men," said the soldier next to Lucifer's corpse. He was the first to notice the pale color and pungent odor. The smell of decaying flatulence filled the air.

After looking at the dead body for a few moments, the soldiers covered Lucifer with a cloak. They had taken it from one of the soldiers who had stayed behind. Resolved to the possibility that the governor might blame them and order their executions, the driver summoned the horses to their previous pace. The driver hoped the governor might perceive their arrival's urgency as evidence of their innocence. The palace was now only a few hundred furlongs away. The estimated time of arrival placed them in the courtyard right before the governor's morning meal.

DAYBREAK

As the sun began to rise, Alexia had already been awake for several moments. Yeshua was just beginning to wake when he noticed that she was no longer lying next to him. At first, he panicked and thought that something might have happened in the darkness of night. Had the soldiers decided to return to the forest and capture her? If so, it did not make sense to only take her without also arresting him. So, Yeshua quickly dismissed the thought.

More painful than the first, a second thought entered his mind as the first thought made its exit. *What if Alexia chose to escape in the night while I was sleeping and return to the comforts of her father's home?* He could neither blame her, nor prevent it from happening. In the real world, family always came first. It was the way things were and had always been. What they were doing felt like an alternate state of reality in a tragic drama. The thought tortured him as his anxiety increased.

He then heard a familiar sound. It was Alexia relieving her body of its excess fluids somewhere nearby. Such an essential bodily function provided such excitement and relief for Yeshua. His initial response was to follow the sound to its source to make sure it was Alexia and not someone else. But, wishing to respect her privacy, Yeshua found a place nearby for his own relief.

The road to Yeriho was lonely. Because it was the most direct path toward Yerushalayim and the temple, most of its travelers, wealthy merchants or devout religious leaders, took the risk despite the danger. Yeshua's narrative about the Ethiopian reflected the greatest fears of most travelers who made the journey. In the story, the Ethiopian rescued the man who had been robbed and left for dead in the ravine. The irony of an Ethiopian performing such a gratuitous act offended many of the Judeans. However, Yeshua wanted people to know that social injustice and prejudices robbed everyone of their basic humanity.

"We are all the man in the ditch," he concluded at the closing of the scene. He recalled the expressions on people's faces as they moved toward the road's main corridor.

After relieving themselves, Alexia and Yeshua moved closer toward the place where the road widened and curved down to the south. The sun's beams slid through the trees and revealed the vestiges of fog and night dew.

"Do you think the soldiers are gone?" Alexia asked.

She desperately needed assurance from Yeshua that it was alright to relax and enjoy the walk. He gave no such assurance. To her surprise, he did not respond at all. He was usually overly attentive to her, especially when she felt anxious.

"Yason," she finally said, "Did you not hear me?"

The whole time Alexia had been looking up at Yeshua, so she never noticed the dark figure standing in the road. Once she looked forward, it became clear why Yeshua said nothing.

DEMETRIS COMETH

Demetris was one of the most fierce and skilled fighters ever known in the Roman army. He stood over eight feet tall. His muscles bulged beneath his breastplate, and he held a sword that weighed the same as the average man. He was legendary for his brutal persecution of Judeans and Roman sympathizers. He was infamous for his gladiatorial exploits in the arena, raids throughout the villages, arrests of Zealots, and he often performed bloody executions at the corner markets in front of the public.

Why was he not with the other soldiers who pursued Yeshua and Alexia the previous night? His lone appearance at the front of the road paralyzed Yeshua. There was no time to process the meaning of Demetris's appearance. Although Yeshua had only seen him once in his life, once was enough to know the inevitable consequences of a confrontation.

After some time, Yeshua was finally able to speak. "Alexia, run back to the village!"

Now it was Alexia's turn to be speechless. She too, became immobilized by the ghostly figure blocking the road.

"Alexia, you must run now!" Yeshua said again with more urgency.

But no amount of emotions awakened her from the trance. Yeshua tried to reason with her, "We will both die here if you do not run."

There was no way to rationalize the moment. Alexia stood frozen as if she had become a pillar of salt.

When he realized that Alexia was not going to run, Yeshua made plans for the best possible outcome. Demetris began to walk swiftly toward them with his sword drawn. His sword moved slowly with each step—from the sidearm position to an overhead stance. Warriors deployed their swords in that manner to obtain the maximum velocity needed to decapitate their opponents.

The technique was so common that young boys often mimicked it using sticks from tree branches. Starting from the hip, the attacker raised the sword in a circular motion high above his head before swiftly severing the head of the unsuspecting victim. He completed the circle by returning the blade to the position beside the hip. It was known to be quick and painless. Most likely, because of her father's clout with the Roman government, Alexia would likely be spared the opportunity to die in such a brutal fashion.

"Peasant. Prepare to die," Demetris yelled as he moved closer to Yeshua and Alexia. "You are an insurrectionist and a murderer. In the name of the emperor Thaddeus, I sentence you to death," he continued without hesitation.

They were sure that death was only seconds away. Yeshua saw Demetris as both messenger and executioner. He had not seriously considered the possibility that the injury inflicted on Lucifer led to her death. For the first time in his life, Yeshua faced the paradox of being both a murderer and a victim in the same scene. Although he had dramatized death, performed the act, and debated the ethics of capital punishment, Yeshua had never imagined himself as the perpetrator. Demetris's words stunned and sobered Yeshua. They distracted him from the reality of what was about to happen, his own death and demise.

While Demetris was rushing towards them and moving his sword in formation, there was a sudden interruption—an intrusive metallic crashing sound. The source of the sound was not apparent to Yeshua, Alexia, or Demetris. Yet, specific facts were obvious. First, Demetris could no longer walk or move his arms. His facial expressions changed from animalistic aggression to pure agony and astonishment.

Second, the sound of broken and cracked bones echoed through the dissipating fog, which made it impossible to comprehend the event entirely. The sound made Yeshua think about the lightning before thunder on those spring nights in Galilee. They were his favorite times as a young boy. The final stage of the dramatic demise of Demetris came with the blade of a foreign sword erupting through the center of his chest, clearly making its entrance from behind and cloaked by the residual fog. The tip of the blade exploded from Demetris's chest and assumed the character of a triumphant demagogue as it twisted and turned before it rescinded into nothingness.

Demetris's lifeless body fell to the ground like an opening curtain in an Athens arena production. It revealed the identity of the culprit. Petras stood center stage with the sword still clenched between his arms and forefingers.

"Petras! What are you doing here?" Yeshua, stunned by the ordeal, said the first thing that came to his mind.

There was no time to be sensitive to Petras's feelings or his. Upon second thought Yeshua wished he had said something to express his gratitude and excitement for Petras's timely appearance. Petras and Yeshua understood the immediacy of the moment, and that they were both functioning on their primal instincts.

"The news is all over the city and villages. Lucifer is dead, and the governor blames you for it. He has sent a bounty for your head," Petras hurriedly explained to Yeshua while he surveyed Demetris's body to make sure life had vacated him. He searched the armor and uniform for possible items that might be useful to Yeshua and Alexia's escape.

"You do not have much time," Petras told them. "Fortunately, I was standing outside the magistrate's office when the order was signed. The soldiers who returned the dead body of Lucifer told Demetris where to find you. The bounty was set at one hundred pieces of silver. As I warmed my hands by the fire, one of the court stewards recognized me from one of the performances.[1] I ran quickly through the courtyard, out the east gate and came directly to intercept Demetris's arrival," Petras explained between gasps for breath. Killing Demetris exhausted him more than wrestling to pull large catches in fishing nets at sea.

Yeshua said to Petras, "We are grateful for your bravery. Are plans still in place for the final performances? Will they still be ready?"

Considering the current events, Yeshua's inquiry surprised Petras. Yet, he admired Yeshua's ability to stay focused on his primary mission.

Petras responded, "Yes, we are ready. However, we had to make a last-minute change. Roman soldiers arrested Yohanan before sunset as he prepared for the evening meal. He was questioned and beaten for several hours but was eventually released to return home to his family. So, we decided it was best not to put the performance at risk."

"Who will take his place?" Yeshua questioned.

"Yael will perform the role of Jesus," said Petras.

Yeshua was quick to react, "Yael! She is a woman. A man has always performed the role of Jesus."

"That is true. I and the others felt that having a woman in that role would send a clear message that the revolution includes all people, not just a few chosen men," Petras argued. His reasoning convinced Yeshua. He was glad to hear Petras stand up for his position and to see his innovative thinking.

"I think it is wonderful," Alexia chimed in.

---

1. Luke 22:54–62.

PETULA'S PLIGHT

In the coming days, the news about the death of Lucifer reverberated throughout the province. The emperor dispensed his fury by raising the bounty even higher than the one set by the governor. Most people did not notice the excessive reaction from the palace, but it came as no surprise to one person, the emperor's wife, for she had known of her husband's exploits for several years.

The public display of his obvious grief over the death of Lucifer was embarrassing. Petula felt overexposed. But what could she do about it? He was the emperor and his power was not to be questioned. As his wife, her life was worth no more than what the emperor granted. So, if he decided she was expendable and no longer of service, he could command her to be put to death at a moment's notice.

Living under the cloak of such power was, at times, overwhelming. At the same time, the advantages and privileges of such a role were more than what any reasonable person could comprehend or resist. The reality of their marriage remained the same: she was only a gift from a wealthy aristocrat of the Roman hierarchy, she was not a person but an exchangeable garment.

So, as they both lay down on the bed where he had laid with many other women and men, the wife of the emperor contemplated her existence in the world. Meanwhile, soldiers who coveted higher rank made plans to go after the man who was responsible for the death of her husband's mistress.

A chime sounded at the main door and signaled a turn of events that startled them both. Because of the proximity, it was difficult to hear the entire conversation between the courier and the concierge. It was clear that Yeshua had not been successfully apprehended and something dreadful had occurred. Thaddeus was first to rise from bed. Unclothed and anxious to hear the news, he reached for a silk cloak laying on the edge of the bed, imported from West Africa, a gift from one of his many wives. It was the last piece of covering that he removed before he went to bed.

"My lord, I am here to report to you the most recent news related to the apprehension of the renegade Yeshua," the courier spoke. "It has been confirmed that Demetris, chief among your royal bounty hunters, was killed in the act of duty."

The courier was very matter of fact and did not show much emotion.

He continued with the report, "The body was discovered by a reconnaissance unit in the area. An obvious intrusion of a sword through the heart from the rear."

As he listened to the message, Thaddeus wondered how Yeshua, an ordinary peasant and street performer, could have mastered such skills against someone of Demetris's military experience.

"We have reissued the bounty and are confident that a more competent person will be dispatched immediately. There is no need to be concerned. This peasant will be arrested, tortured, and put to death. My lord, I beg you to return to bed and let us deal with this matter," the courier said, trying to reassure him.

Thaddeus interrupted, "I want your best men placed on immediate search and seizure. Surely, the peasant did not act alone. I want to know who helped him."

"Yes, my lord. It shall be done as you command," the soldier said without ever relinquishing his formal posture.

Thaddeus continued, "And, I want additional forces dispatched to the Yeriho road. Whoever is with him must not get far."

Thaddeus was oblivious to Yeshua's company. He was unaware that the daughter of a prominent Roman citizen conspired in the escape. Furthermore, no one knew the intimate details of Alexia and Yeshua's relationship, except for the one that was now dead. One could only imagine what would happen if Thaddeus knew.

"My lord, if I may offer a suggestion," the soldier asked while standing at attention.

"Yes, you may speak," Thaddeus said.

"There has been word that another performance will take place in a few days. The fugitive may still be in proximity to the province. We can place men at all the gates in case he tries to reenter the city. We should not assume he is going to run away," the soldier sputtered and continued to wait for a response from the emperor.

"What you say is possible. I will accept your suggestion and add it to my order," Thaddeus concurred.

Thaddeus was surprised that he had not thought of that possibility. Not wanting to show any sign of weakness, the emperor gave a stern command, "That will be all for now. You have your orders. I do not want to see you standing before me again without this peasant in your custody."

"It will be done, my lord," the soldier responded.

Trying not to show the worry in his voice, the captain knew the fates of those who failed the emperor. It was no time to show vulnerability. After offering the formal salute to Thaddeus, the soldier retreated to the corridor leading out to the main courtyard. His chariot and horses, in formation, awaited their next commands.

As the soldier approached his chariot, he summoned the other men to follow him out of the palace gate. He resolved to tell them about the commitments he made on their behalf once they were near the main gate.

At that moment, pageantry was more important than reality. Failure was not an option to be entertained by the legion. Each chariot, with two men and two horses, began exiting in rank order. Thaddeus stood high above them on the upper terrace. He felt confident about the demonstration of military discipline as he watched each chariot leave in proper fashion.

THADDEUS'S FURY

Thaddeus was furious about the news of the deaths of Lucifer and Demetris. In the coming days, he sent out a series of edicts, new curfews, and warrants for anyone who conspired or associated with the fugitives. Despite questions about Yeshua's participation in armed resistance, Thaddeus was shocked that things had come to such a violent conclusion.

"All this bloodshed over a few silly dramas in the streets, simple-minded peasant stories designed to entertain the masses and distract them from their labors. It does not make sense to me," Thaddeus spoke out loud to himself as he placed his stamp on the final warrant. "Perhaps I am overreacting to nothing."

Suddenly his wife appeared in the room unannounced. "You are not overreacting. You are the supreme emperor of all time. You must show no sign of weakness. I have witnessed one of his dramas. They provoke violence and civil disobedience among the unlearned. He encouraged a disregard for authority and often mocked his religious leaders and their gods. Such a person cannot be tolerated or allowed to live freely," Petula said.

"Yes, my dear, you are right. But something still appears to be unresolved. Although the insurrection was discovered and its leader banished from the province, I still feel that his presence is very much alive among the villagers. Silencing the man does not always guarantee that you are silencing the myth. The investigation must continue as the warrants are sent to the magistrates. I must find out how this man's performances became so popular. Total submission to the will of the empire must be secured. Anything less will not be tolerated," said Thaddeus.

Thaddeus's wife, being more supportive than usual, moved closer behind him and wrapped her arms around his waist, and stroked his chest.

"I support you and all that you are," she said. "I praise the gods for you and the gift that is bursting within you. You are the greatest emperor ever known to Rome. The people love you, and any man will give his life to protect your name. You are the true son of god and none other will ever be greater."

Thaddeus was comforted by her words, but he did not fully trust this rare patronage. He wondered silently about her true motives. It could not be sex because he had provided for that. He wondered whether she was relieved by the death of her main rival, the only person who had ever threatened her grip on his heart. He first thought to question her motives, but later decided that her comforting presence was more valuable to him than having a marital spat.

"I will capture the street performer and his treacherous companion and return them to be made examples before the people of the village," Thaddeus declared as he looked out an open window facing the outer terrace. "No one man is above the law and he will be held accountable. It will be the last of this matter and the people can return to a peaceful state. Yeshua has lied to his own people, making them think that the order of the universe is not as it has always been. The first thing I will do will be to call a meeting of their religious leaders and ask their assistance in reeducating the people. I will ask for the help of Josephus. He has always been a reliable ally in keeping the status quo. But I will not include Nicodemus this time. In our last meeting, he did not seem as supportive as he has been in the past. There is something different about him."

Thaddeus turned and gave his wife a firm embrace. Feeling more confident about his plan to bring matters under control had aroused him. They kissed passionately while embracing each other.

Chapter 12

Performances

THE NINTH HOUR WAS quickly approaching as the sun rested at its highest point in the sky. The calm before the storm settled over the province. People flooded into the marketplace.

Petras returned to prepare for the final performance. The other actors had assembled at Matthew's home in the lower east side of the village. Short of the remoteness of Yeshua's farmhouse, it was the perfect meeting place. Matthew's house was a small mudflat that receded into the side of a hill. Those in the vicinity would not be apt to notice it unless they knew of its existence. Matthew had inherited the home from his father's brother and was fond of the quiet and reclusive home that provided a perfect space to practice his writing skills—something had been handed down by the men in the family, as his father and grandfather were professional scribes.

Most of the central actors who were in the final performance had gathered early that morning. Four people rehearsed the role of Jesus. The decision to cast Yael in the role provoked brief discussion among the men, but most favored the idea, if for no other reason than its strategic advantage. Most Romans were less threatened by females, and because of her age, people would not likely take the performance seriously. The simple fact, however, remained: any portrayal of a Judean Messiah, executed by the Roman government, would provoke the emperor's wrath and draw a violent reaction regardless of who performed the role.

When Petras finally reached the house, he knocked on the door using the coded cadence established by The Ekklesia. Matthew opened the window in the door first to double-check that an imposter had not invaded their group.

"It is me, Petras. I am alone," he yelled.

Petras's identification of himself assured Matthew it was safe to let him in the house. He opened the door, and Petras quickly entered the front room where the others sat. The room was dark, making it difficult to recognize every person in the space among the twenty or so actors gathered.

"We were beginning to worry about you. You look exhausted," Matthew said.

Petras replayed the events of the night when he killed Demetris, the Roman bounty hunter. "I did not have any time to waste and did not return to my home. I ran here directly and made sure no one saw me," he explained.

"There has been much speculation about who killed Demetris," said Yael.

She worked in the market most mornings and was privy to the gossip of the villagers. Yael's work helped her gain valuable information, but it also ensured she maintained a routine as she did not want to draw unwanted attention.

"Most people think it was Yason," said Yael. "But I also heard another person say Yason probably had an accomplice. Many soldiers have been patrolling the markets, and most of them seem disinterested in finding out who murdered one of theirs."

"We must not let any of this discourage us. The performances will take place as planned," Petras announced to the group. "The more people in the markets and village squares the better—the message will be communicated. Let us remember why we are doing this: not for fortune or for fame, but for the people. So that every woman and man, girl and boy, will know the truth. Only the truth will set our people free.

"What is this truth, you ask?" Petras asked rhetorically.

"Tell us, Petras," Marco yelled with anticipation from the back of the room.

"The truth that will set our minds free from the past," said Petras. "The truth that our oppressors are the Roman Empire. This empire exploits us by occupying our land and keeping us divided against each other. This empire tells us that we are not born free people. It teaches that our history of enslavement is the inevitable consequence of the sins of our mothers and fathers—that we are slaves in our own land, with no rights and no right to self-determination. But we know that is not true." By now, Petras spoke in a rhythmic cadence like the prophets of old.

"Tell us the truth Petras," Yael shouted.

"This city was built on the backs of our brothers and sisters. The streets of this city were paved with the blood of our mothers and our fathers. We shall overcome this oppression because our leader, Yeshua, has shown us the way. He has taught us that we are stronger together than we are apart. The Judean, the Greek, the Asiatic, the Muslim, the Barbarian are all family and we can coexist. No one person is free as long as any person is enslaved."

Petras paused as a frenzied spirit filled the room.

He continued, "As that great martyr foretold, 'When the spirit of the time has fully come, the young will see new visions and the old will dream dreams. Your sons and your daughters,'" Petras paused and looked directly at Yael. "They will proclaim this truth."

The entire room became engulfed by the spirit of the ancestors. They sang and chanted in the secret language of the oppressed. Petras swayed with the rhythm of the room and appeared to be in a trance. Some of the younger actors beat on their drums with the palm of their hands, carefully keeping the sound to a minimum.

The women began to dance in response to the spirit. An Ethiopian woman, known by the name Baraka, suddenly broke out in a song that featured a guttural roll of the tongue. All attention was on her beautiful bronze body, clothed with a silk cloak of Egyptian red thread—a sign of royal class distinction. Her vocal inflections passionately expressed the pain and grief of oppressed people.

As the meeting reached its natural conclusion, Petras offered a final exhortation, "Let us prepare ourselves for the moment that is to come," he said.

He then reached into his shoulder bag for the pouch of leftover wine from the last rehearsal at Yeshua's home. He lifted it high above his head as a symbolic gesture of their communal sacrifice.

"Drink this wine and bread as if it will be your last. Always remember the words of our founder and leader, Yason. May his legacy live on in us all," he spoke.

"It is so and shall be," the people responded in unison.

Many in the room started to speculate about whether Yeshua was still alive or dead. Some wondered if Petras was candid with them.

Nathan, one of the performers whose task was to secure the mules for the parade in the streets, quietly whispered to Yael, "It is rumored that Petras killed Yeshua and now wants to take credit for this work. Is this true?"

Yael remained quiet. She did not want to attract attention. "Leave me alone," Yael scoffed and whispered. "I am a servant of the narrative that will separate the wheat from the chaff in this city. It does not matter to me or anyone else the true motives of Petras. All I know is that the time is right for us to realize that things are not as they should be. We have become too dependent on the Romans for our protection, our identity as a people, and even our religion. Yeshua showed us through his dramatic performances that the word of God is alive in us with a message of liberation. We cannot deny this truth."

By the time she finished speaking, serene pools of tears illuminated Yael's dark eyes.

Nathan appeared to be moved by the words from Yael. Although not a religious man, he remained convinced that helping to make the performances successful was worth the risk of being arrested by the Romans. As planned, he proceeded to prepare for Yael to ride into the center of the city market. He was unaware of the ancient stories that described a new king riding down the streets of the city on a mule.

The atmosphere in the room was calm as everyone quietly moved to their respective places. Petras announced that Yeshua was on the run with Alexia. Yet, the report of her father's execution early that morning had not reached her. A group of servants loyal to the emperor decapitated him and his wife, two of her brothers, and the escorts assigned to watch Alexia. The news of the killing of a prominent Roman family solidified in the hearts of all the actors that this performance could be their final act—with no redemptive purpose. They still felt compelled to proceed with the plans.

YAEL'S PERFORMANCE

The midday crowd was astonished at Yael's presence on the mule as she slowly made her way through the market. Fully draped with a grayish shroud that covered most of her body, no one knew her true identity. Her athletic body cloaked her femininity. The mule strolled into the city square, where thousands had gathered with great anticipation. Most assumed it was Yeshua. Rumors had spread that he might make an appearance in the place closest within view of the emperor's palace. Yael's head moved up and down in sync with the movement of the mule's steps.

Despite the fact that Yael had been the most supportive of the movement to free the minds of the people from the beginning, it remained difficult for her to absorb the moment. Those chosen to play extras began their initial chants.

"Hosanna, the king cometh!" those who were a part of the crowd yelled.

They lined up along the road toward the center market, being true to the tradition, and laid down palm branches. Yael's heart beat faster and faster as she moved along the path. She was careful not to remove her shawl and reveal her identity.

Amid the excitement, the absence of Yeshua saddened Yael. He taught her so much about portraying a foreign character and projecting their essence in a dramatic fashion. She thought about how insecure she had been when it all first began. Yeshua inspired her to reach deep within and pull out the confidence that she needed to perform.

But this was no mere performance. The events that were about to unfold were as real as water. Yael panicked as the pace of her heartbeat quickened to allow for maximum adrenaline flow. No amount of rehearsal or memorization could prepare her for what was to happen shortly.

Yael had a vision of Yeshua speaking softly in her ear. It was not an unfamiliar recollection. He had done so many times during rehearsals to help her get into character. Now the experience was surreal. She could feel him saying as clearly as she could hear her heartbeat, "It is for such a time as this you came into this world."

No one could have predicted, not even Yael, what happened next. Slowly, she reached up over her head and removed the hood. It became clear that the person performing the role of the most significant social force of the times was a young brown woman riding into the center of public appraisal, with poise and confidence.

Everyone was surprised to see it was Yael, proudly adorning Egyptian braids dangling down her back. The women suddenly stopped laying down the palm branches, and the people in the audience who had joined in with the chanting ceased immediately. There was a poignant silence in the air, which allowed a more audible sound of the mule's hoofs.

Yael thought, *I will be killed for sure, if not by the Romans, then by my own people for such mockery of the tradition.*

Despite inevitable scrutiny, Yael continued to move toward the central plaza to be greeted by the actors in fabricated Roman soldier attire.

Two actual soldiers mounted on horses were waiting and prepared to arrest Yeshua on the scene. But they were unprepared for what occurred. The soldiers were baffled and looked at one another to clarify how best to handle the situation. The more senior leader spoke.

"Our orders were to arrest the renegade, Yeshua," he said. "This is not him. It is only a woman. Let us return in rank. There is no threat here."

The other soldier appeared to agree and returned his sword to its sheath. "We will report what our eyes have witnessed," he announced.

So, they rode off on horses as people in the crowd noticed and began to laugh and cheer.

"God has given us hope for tomorrow through this brave woman," an older male bystander spoke loudly. Others around him joined in agreement, "It is so and shall be."

Once the mule arrived at the center square, Yael dismounted without hesitation and raised her arms in the air over her head. Those acting as soldiers were confused by the unrehearsed gesture. Therefore, they both remained still in their position until Yael gave them a sign.

Yael, overwhelmed by the spirit of the moment, found words flowing out of her mouth extemporaneously. The other actors stood quietly in their places. As she held one hand in the air, fist clenched as a sign of defiance, she heeded the moment and spoke with a loud voice. She uttered these words:

> "Behold, the handmaiden of my Lord. My soul does magnify the
> Lord of all Lords.[1] The mighty one has done good things. Adonai
> is full of mercy, bringing rulers down from their thrones and
> lifting the humble. The spirit is upon me and has anointed me to
> announce good news from The Ekklesia. To bring comfort to the
> afflicted and proclaim liberation to all who are oppressed. Today
> is the day. This is the year of Adonai's holy reign!"

A sudden silence hovered over the crowd as many were shocked at what they just witnessed. Some were familiar with the words of the great prophet but had never imagined them spoken by a woman—especially a woman of Yael's status. Everyone stood in silence while they took in the meaning of her performance. Above all, they feared what the Roman soldiers might do. How would they interpret the meaning and intent of the prophet's words?

Artemis, the captain over the legion, stood motionless as Yael continued repeating the last reframe of her impromptu speech.

"This is the year," she emphatically declared.

Without much warning or forethought, Artemis lifted his hand high in the air and slowly pointed his index finger directly at Yael and the mule. Twenty paces away, his chief archery man already had his bow aimed at the intended target. He released it from its nocked position. It struck Yael with the force of ten horses, knocked her to the ground, and spared the mule. The crowd gasped. Some ran for fear of their own lives. Most stood still so that none of the soldiers mistook their actions for rioting.

Yael lay on the ground with her arms extended outward from her body. Artemis walked over to her, reached down to break off the end of the bow, and extubated it from her chest. Blood and water gushed from her open wound.

1. Luke 1:46–55.

"Not today," Artemis said as he walked away to leave her lifeless body bleeding on the street.

PETRAS'S PERFORMANCE

The situation for Petras was much different than that of Yael's. The municipal square was located within the eye of the Roman Centerplex where the coliseum and judicial courts were in session. Because of the Passover holiday, most Judeans rested at home or gathered at the village square near the markets.

As Petras rode on his mule toward the square, he assumed that the other actors had reached their destinations. By now, the Roman soldiers knew there was more than one performance, and Yeshua was not at any of the previous ones.

Like Yael, Petras arrived wrapped in a cloak, and a hood covered his face. The supporting cast members lined the street and shouted, "Hosanna." However, they were previously instructed not to respond, "Here comes our king," until Petras's mule came to a halt at the heart of the square.

Surprisingly, this crowd was the largest among the other three performances, probably because of the anticipation that Yeshua would be arrested and executed on the spot. Petras was not sure whether Thaddeus had discovered that he was the one who murdered the bounty hunter and helped Yeshua escape.

As the mule moved slowly toward the square, it swayed with the rhythm of the moment—with calm and grace. Petras thought, "This poor beast does not realize that it is carrying a man to his death."

Many Roman citizens or sympathizers laughed out loud at the sight of the man on the mule. None of them were aware of the prophecy. It was merely entertainment. Nothing about it represented a threat to the lordship of the emperor.

The journey into the square seemed to take an eternity. As the mule kept its steady pace, Petras found time to reminisce about the first time he met Yeshua. He had just docked his fishing boat with the assistance of his brother Andrew. The catch was small that day because of the tides. A night storm had left the sea active and challenging to maneuver. Andrew, the younger of the two, recalled seeing a vision of a man walking on water toward their boat. Although he dismissed the image as a combination of too much wine and the rough seas, Petras also saw a similar sight the previous week and wondered if it was a sign of things to come.

Regardless of the meaning of the vision, meeting Yeshua that day reminded Petras of the vision. Like the stranger walking on the sea, Yeshua walked up to Petras's boat to help Andrew and him bring it to the shore.

"How was your catch for the night?" Yeshua asked. "It does not look as if you were very successful." The light weight of the boat made it obvious the catch was minimal.

"You are correct. The storms made the waters too difficult for fishing. But there is always tomorrow. What do you know about fishing?" Petras inquired.

"Not much, my friend. But I like to come to the shore to watch the fisherman returning with their boats. I have done this since I was a young boy. You can always look at the expression on their faces and tell how good the catch was the night before. It is that look of dread or satisfaction that tells the whole story," Yeshua explained.

"You are very observant, my young friend," Petras said. "But it does not tell the whole story. Being a good fisherman is more than about how many fish you catch. It is about being on the sea and learning that you are not always in control of your life. It only takes one unexpected roar of the sea to cause the waves to turn your boat in the wrong direction away from the fish. One must have a lot of patience and skill to be a good fisherman."

Petras's description of life on the sea was accurate. Entire cultures of commerce would be defined by ships' movement along the southern routes toward Northern Africa. The ships like the corsairs would rule the oceans for centuries.

"I see what you mean. Life in these parts is always unpredictable. We Judeans are never in control of our destiny," Yeshua said. The words seemed to touch a chord within Petras and piqued his interest.

"So, are you a politician or a Zealot?" Petras asked. "If so, we don't want anything to do with you. Life on the sea is dangerous enough. I do not want to die on land because of conversing with a subversive radical."

"You have nothing to worry about, my friend," Yeshua responded. "I am neither."

"Who are you?" Petras asked.

"Who am I, you ask?" Yeshua seemed surprised by Petras's question. "I am the son of Samuel and Miriam."

"So, you are a peasant farmer?" Petras sarcastically responded. "A farmer who spends his time watching fisherman. Does this mean you want to be one of us?"

"Of course not," Yeshua replied. "I was wondering if you wanted to become one of us."

Petras was confused by the conversation. Why would he want to become a farmer? Farmers were the lowest rung on the social hierarchy ladder. The only thing worse was being a pig farmer.

"A farmer? Why would I want to lower myself in such a way?" Peter asked.

Yeshua suddenly laughed, which confused and frustrated Petras. He thought, *Why am I wasting my time having a conversation that I don't even care to have*? He felt repulsed by Yeshua, yet also drawn to him. He seemed different from other men that Petras knew, seemingly so resolved and confident in himself.

"I am more than a farmer," Yeshua finally said. "My father owns one of the largest farms in the province and has customers from the highest ranks among the Romans. But not only that. I am a mason and carpenter by trade, and a street performer too."

"A performer?" Petras asked. "What is that?"

Yeshua knew he had captured Petras's interest. He was quick to reply. "I perform small scenes on the streets and in the public square. My performances tell stories and parables about life and new possibilities. I have a company of followers who assist me. We are growing fast because our message gives people hope that God has not abandoned them and that one day, we will be free of the Romans."

"It is dangerous to hope for such things," Petras said. "You can get in trouble for arousing the people's hope for desires that cannot be fulfilled."

"Yes, it is dangerous work. That's why I perform parables with riddles that are only understandable to our people. Only the poor can understand them. The rich are too preoccupied with staying rich and gaining more power. My performances show people the truth," Yeshua expounded. "You must come to see one of my performances. We will be performing at the market square tomorrow morning before the sun peaks. Since you will not return to the sea for another three days and your fish will not be selling in the markets, it should not be a problem for you to come. I promise you will like it. If so, consider joining us."

Petras made a slight expression of doubt on his face, "And why should I consider that?" he queried.

"Because it is obvious that you and your brother are not very good fishermen. Come with me, and I will make you fishers of men," Yeshua avowed while gazing directly into the eyes of Petras.

Petras never forgot that day. He did just as Yeshua proposed. He went and saw the performance and never returned to fishing in the sea.

He was awakened to the present moment by the shouts of the crowds. "Hosanna! Hosanna!" they screamed. Petras knew the implications of his

actions. In a moment of sobriety, he hesitated inside and questioned himself. *What am I doing here? What is this all about?* His mind began to explore
all options for how he could vacate the moment. *How did I go from being a
lonely fisherman to a murderer facing his demise?*

It was then that he heard the voice of Yeshua speaking:

> *You are here because of something bigger than yourself,*
> *the truth through the ages is telling you*
> *that the current state of affairs is not just,*
> *and people are dying silently behind a veil of oppression.*
> *Who will speak the truth*
> *while innocent children and their mothers*
> *are led to the slaughter?*
> *Who will speak the truth*
> *when young girls and boys are born*
> *into slavery in their own land,*
> *never to imagine freedom?*
> *Who will speak the truth?*
> *The truth is that our leaders have sold us*
> *for thirty pieces of silver.*
> *Petras, will you speak the truth?*

Petras abruptly felt arrested by the spirit of the times. He felt God's
presence all around him. For some unknown reason, he was no longer
afraid.

"Let thy will be done," he whispered as the mule came to an unanticipated stop.

Even the mule sensed the presence of something—he became violently
agitated and began to jump up and down. Petras was quick to jump with the
mule until their bodies were perfectly synchronized. When the timing was
perfect, Petras used the inertia of the mule's movements to leap into the air.
He propelled himself up and away from the frightened animal. He landed
on both feet and then removed the cloak that masked his face.

The Roman soldiers were already moving toward the commotion
caused by the mule's behavior. Still, they were immediately bewildered
when they noticed that the one who rode the mule was not Yeshua. The one
whom they were looking for was easily recognizable for his physical presence—he was taller than most men, had extremely dark skin, and long curly
hair. More than any other feature, Yeshua was known for his hazel-colored
eyes, an anomaly for Judeans. Petras had none of those features. He was
short, had reddish hair, and was light-skinned. He was often called Ruddy

or Fiery Red, not only for his appearance but also because of his impulsive personality.

Confused about what to do, the soldiers looked to each other for a solution. Intuitively, they both reached the same conclusion. It would be far better to return to the emperor with a suspect than to appear empty-handed. So, they motioned to each other to proceed with making an arrest. At least they were arresting someone who was smaller and appeared to be less of a threat.

Neither was aware that they attempted to subdue the man who had murdered the most dangerous man in the province a day earlier. Petras observed every move and mentally anticipated each step made by the soldiers. He knew his arrest was imminent, and death by execution would soon follow.

As they came closer to him, he offered no signs of resistance. It would have been useless to do so. He did not have his sword with him. He briefly imagined how he would have cut off one of the soldiers' ears to symbolize the government's unwillingness to listen to the common people's concerns and sufferings.

Some of the other actors were surprised by the soldiers' sudden intrusion—especially the two actors standing in those parts. They stood motionless as the actual Roman soldiers, in their authentic military wardrobe, seized Petras, secured both arms behind his back, and shackled him in iron restraints.

When the crowd saw the irons, they knew that the arrest was real and not part of the production. The metal's unique quality was a distinct production of the Judean blacksmiths but not licensed for use by the peasantry. Petras offered no resistance to the soldiers, which angered them because it disappointed their hopes for a more dramatic performance.

As Petras was herded away in a wagon, the people in the crowds returned to their chant, "Hosanna."[2]

But this time, they added, "To the king."

2. Matt 21:1–9.

Chapter 13

Resurrection

BY MIDDAY, ALEXIA AND Yeshua arrived in Yeriho, a vibrant city situated beyond the Jordan, west of the City of Peace. Making the journey only during daylight hours took a few days because of frequent stops for water and rest. As a child, Yeshua made the trip several times with his father on foot and by mule. He relished the regal cultural atmosphere, with its eclectic market smells and fragrances, imported spices, and meats from worldwide. It would be safer for them here, where the emperor's reach was minimal. The diversity of thoughts, cultures, and religions made Yeriho a hub of creativity.

As they entered the city's main gate, one of the most fortified cities in the region, Yeshua and Alexia's bodies seemed to relax. But relaxing caused other basic physical sensations in their bodies, like hunger and fatigue, to become more noticeable. It was also the busiest time of the day. People of all persuasions and motivations filled the streets in a flurried attempt to close the day with a profit.

"I am hungry, my love. Can we find something to eat?" Alexia asked, exhausted from the trip.

"Don't worry. I know just the place to go for fresh food. Follow me."

Yeshua spoke with his head turned toward his back. It was the first time he realized that Alexia traveled behind him. He felt terrible for not previously noticing. He was often unaware that most people were not his height and their legs were not as long as his. Alexia needed to take three steps to keep up with one of his. "Forgive me for walking so fast. My mind is preoccupied with many things. I did not notice that I was leaving you behind." Yeshua began to slow down his pace, a courtesy Alexia appreciated.

"I am fine, Yeshua. I can keep up with you and any other man," Alexia insisted as she picked up her pace.

"Just around the corner is a place my father often took us to for a quick meal," Yeshua said. "We will be safe here. People here only worry about their own affairs. News from the valley seldom reaches here. If so, nobody really cares."

Another reason that he liked Yeriho came to mind—the mountains. They surrounded the road leading to the city from the valley. Once they reached the heart of the town, Yeshua and Alexia turned around to look at the winding road that led to Yeriho. It reminded Yeshua of a natural amphitheatre, similar to the ones he dreamed of performing in most of his life.

"On stage, I can be whoever I want to be," he would say to himself.

In the evenings, if you walked around in the market's center, looking toward the mountains, then you would hear the echo of your footsteps in the air. As a youth, Yeshua stood in the center square and imagined being a famous actor, known worldwide, who performed in large arenas.

Being back in the city was a momentary distraction for Yeshua from their current crisis. First and foremost, he needed to find a secure location for Alexia and him to stay for a few days. They also needed food. Alexia appeared content with the wait, but Yeshua insisted that finding safe lodging be their top priority. Yeshua led Alexia to a hostel on the north end of the town. It was a place where his father often stayed during business trips to the market.

Named Beit Shalom, it had a reputation for being a refuge for foreign travelers entering the city. There were countless stories of people who had been beaten and robbed on the road and were taken to the hostel to receive care. Often the owners guaranteed at least three nights of complimentary lodging for those who had fallen into such misfortune.

The owners of the Beit Shalom were an old married couple named Benrudah and Abigail. They had acquired the hostel when the Romans took over the province. Many of the stone buildings were destroyed by multiple wars during the occupation. Those left standing were made available for purchase to anyone who could afford to pay the local government's tax allocation. Benrudah was a shrewd businessman who made his fortune selling iron scraps to the Roman army. Abigail owned a seamstress business and accumulated a lot of clients during the festival seasons. With their combined resources, they paid the taxes, bought the land rights to the property, and opened the hostel several years ago.

"I know just the place where we can find shelter," Yeshua said to Alexia as he began walking toward the north end.

"Are you sure we will be safe?" Alexia asked.

"Yes," Yeshua said, and he gave more details as they walked toward the hostel. "My father knows the owner, and they are very good people. I trust them totally."

"I trust you, my love," Alexia reminded him.

It did not take long for them to reach the north end. The hostel was a small stone building with a wooden sign above the entrance saying, "Beit Shalom." Two cypress trees stood on the side of the wooden door that led to the main entrance. Only a couple of people were moving in and around the building. It seemed quiet and safe. There was a noticeable absence of Roman authority in the city. Yeshua wondered whether the emperor transferred resources to another town or if there was a simple disinterest in the affairs of Yeriho. He hoped the truth was the latter. He and Alexia walked through the hostel's open door.

"Yeshua, son of Samuel!" A loud voice bellowed from behind the front counter.

Benrudah immediately recognized the young boy who always came to the city with his father. In those days, Yeshua had not begun the rapid growth spurt most boys experienced at puberty. Despite his size, Yeshua always worked closely with his father to carry heavy loads of preserved meats. The pork had been soaked in salt from the Dead Sea and stored in large burlap sacks.

Benrudah not only provided a place for them to stay while they did business in the town's market, but he was also one of Samuel's best customers. The Beit Shalom hostel provided meals for its guests, who preferred seasoned pork, especially the skins. Proper meats were also available for the local Judean guests. Benrudah could not believe how much young Yeshua had grown as he now stood over six feet tall. He had become a handsome Judean man.

"I cannot believe my eyes. Look at you. You look like an Egyptian prince," Benrudah said as he walked from behind the desk.

Despite being much shorter in stature than Yeshua, he nevertheless was intent on hugging and kissing him. Yeshua anticipated the height difference, so he bent over and made himself accessible to Benrudah's embrace.

"You look just like your father," Benrudah said as he finished kissing Yeshua and pushed back from him to get a better look.

"No, he looks like his mother," his wife Abigail declared with a loud voice as she appeared from another room in the back of the hostel.

Her happiness to see Yeshua was equal to her husband's. She also engaged in the same ritual of hugging and kissing but quickly turned her attention to Alexia, who stood quietly behind Yeshua.

"So, Yeshua, who is this beautiful young woman? Are you married now?" she asked. "Your father said nothing about you being married the last time he was here. By the way, where is your father? He and Miriam have not been to town for the last few months. Have they found a new business in another town?"

Abigail continued to ask questions without allowing much time for Yeshua to respond, which relieved him because it gave him more time to come up with thoughtful answers.

"Abigail, the boy just arrived," Benrudah interrupted. "Let us be better hosts and let him and his new bride get some rest."

He said this not only to show hospitality but also to manipulate the situation to have time alone with Yeshua. Benrudah said, "Come now," motioning to Abigail, "take the young bride upstairs so that she can pick a room for them. Yeshua and I are going out on the terrace to catch up."

Abigail wished to avoid the appearance of being disrespectful. Her usual response would have been to continue with her inquiry, but she noticed the look in Benrudah's eyes when he ordered them to go upstairs. It was a look of urgency. It was the look that she had seen before whenever travelers came who needed immediate refuge, and there was no time to give lengthy explanations. It was the look that said, "I know something you do not know, and I need you to trust that I know what I am doing." So instead of protesting, Abigail yielded to her husband's wishes.

"Come with me, my dear, and we will find the best room for you and your husband," Abigail instructed Alexia. "Then we will prepare a delectable meal."

As Benrudah and Yeshua walked out onto the terrace, the ocean view was breathtaking. With the view of the mountains, nothing felt more secure than being in Yeriho with familiar friends. Benrudah invited Yeshua to recline on a stone chaise that faced the ocean.

"Come, Yeshua rest yourself here while we talk," Benrudah requested. Yeshua complied with Benrudah's directions and welcomed his hospitality. Benrudah continued to talk.

"I cannot tell you enough how much it warms my heart to see you," he said. "You were a young lad the last time I saw you. Your father always talked about you when he came to do business. He is so proud of you. He says you remind him so much of himself. Strong, smart, and wanting so much to make a difference in the world for his people."

Yeshua was surprised and touched by the things he shared. He never realized his father thought these things about him. Feelings of both adoration and frustration filled his heart as they talked. Although it felt good to hear the positive things his father expressed about him, he resented not hearing them directly.

He did not want Benrudah to know his true thoughts, so Yeshua simply responded, "Thank you, sir, for your hospitality. I am grateful for the chance to be here and to know that my father holds these thoughts towards me."

"No need, my son. Your father and I are like brothers. Therefore, you are like a nephew to me," Benrudah said as he reclined on the other stone chaise next to Yeshua. One of his servants delivered two wine chalices. Then the female quickly disappeared back into the hostel.

"My son, we have to talk," said Benrudah. "I know why you are here and what is going on in the empire. You are in trouble. You have to trust me."

Yeshua, startled by this revelation, remarked, "Thank you, sir. But I do not want to bother you with my troubles."

"It is no trouble," Benrudah insisted, "You are family, and I can protect you here until it is safe for you to move further down the coast. I know many people who can help you. It is no trouble for me."

"Thank you for your willingness to help. You are gracious," Yeshua said. "What did my father tell you?"

Yeshua could not resist asking the question for two reasons. First, he wanted to know how accurate or even truthful his father had been about the circumstances. After their last conversation, there was no mutual understanding of the events that led to his decision to relocate. Second, since being on the road to Yeriho, they had not heard anything about the consequences of the performances. Most likely, his father had either been present at one of the performances or heard a word about what happened—perhaps from one of his business partners who frequented the market. Not knowing what happened to his friends had been the most difficult part of being so far away. It still seemed unbelievable to think that the character of Jesus had become a cultural juggernaut.

"Your father tells me that things are chaotic around the governor's palace," Benrudah spoke slowly between sips of wine. He took a long moment to gulp down a mouthful before he continued. "The performances of your company were interrupted by the Roman soldiers. The fisherman Petras was taken into custody, questioned, and released. His actions posed no threat to the emperor."

"What about Yohanan and James?" Yeshua asked.

"Your father did not mention them," Benrudah answered, "But there was one execution."

"Who was it?" Yeshua frantically queried.

"A young thespian called . . . Yael?" Benrudah said as if he was not sure that he had the correct name. "It is not clear why she was there and how she became a target."

Yeshua's heart sank into his stomach at the news of Yael's death. Benrudah kept talking, oblivious about the impact on Yeshua.

"It appears no harm has come to your friends," he continued. "It is you the emperor wants for the death of his Lieutenant Lucifer and the bounty hunter Demetris. Your father is concerned for your safety and your life. If we can get you and your wife on a ship, you will be safe and start a new life. Do not worry. I know people beyond the empire's reach who can help you get resettled."

"How are my father and my mother? Did the messenger say?" Yeshua asked.

"Your father and mother are fine for now. They are worried about you. The emperor will not harm them because your father's meats are too important to the Roman elite. It is all about resources. Your father has economic security. After a while, no one will even remember you or your silly performances," Benrudah said with a smile as he took a sip of wine.

The words were difficult as well as comforting to hear. Yeshua both wanted his work to have a lasting impression on the people, but the lure of anonymity was far more attractive at that moment. Many thoughts and questions raced through Yeshua's mind, but he did not think they were worth asking. Surely his father had no concern about the dramas.

"Your father told me something else to share with you," Benrudah seemed to read the expression on Yeshua's face.

"What is that, sir?"

Benrudah leaned closer and placed his hand on Yeshua's left shoulder. "He said, 'Tell my son I am proud of what he has done for his people. Let him know I was in the crowd at the performance by Petras. Although he was taken away before the end of the scene, the people were moved by his bravery and commitment. He calmly allowed the soldiers to take him away without any resistance. He will be remembered for what happened.'"

Yeshua wanted very much to share in Benrudah's optimism about Petras's performance. But he could not for reasons that he did not think Benrudah could understand. He did not know how to inquire about the questions he had in his mind. So far, there had been no mention of the final scene in which the character Jesus was taken into Roman custody and executed.

Yeshua thought about the many debates he had with Petras about the significance of the death of Jesus. It was essential to the character's evolution not to be another messiah who led a military campaign. As Benrudah talked about the performances, Yeshua listened to learn if there was any word about a death scene. Indeed, such a scene would have been an embarrassment to the emperor's facade of benevolence.

Yeshua was unsure about how Benrudah would respond to such an inquiry. It was dubious that Benrudah would comprehend since he was traditional in his beliefs and ideas and, like most Judeans, rejected the concept of the tragic hero in Greek mythology.

"Yes, your father was very impressed with the performance," Benrudah finally said. "He never realized the size of following this Jesus man had until the performance by Petras. When he arrived at the main square near the emperor's palace, your father was amazed at the large crowds of people from various backgrounds. Yes, son, you are right about your father's apprehensiveness about your work. Yet, when your father saw how excited the people were about your dramas, he felt so proud to tell everyone who listened to him that his son authored the stories."

"Thank you, sir. It means a great deal to me to know my father approves," Yeshua remarked. He hoped this would motivate Benrudah to share more. Another sip of the wine seemed to be the only incentive Benrudah needed to keep divulging details.

"You are welcome, my son," Benrudah said. "More than anything, your father was relieved that you are still alive."

The news about the performances by Petras and Yael deeply saddened Yeshua. It was his hope and dream that the death of Jesus would inspire others to offer their lives as a sacrifice for the sake of liberation from the Roman Empire. Also, he hoped having Jesus killed at the hands of Roman soldiers would send a clear message that Thaddeus was an unjust ruler who would go to all lengths to suppress the truth of the Judean situation.

Yeshua suddenly felt himself sink into a depressed state. As Benrudah continued to chatter about the heroism of the Jesus man, Yeshua drank the remaining wine in his chalice.

"So, have you two solved all of the world's problems?" Alexia said as she and Abigail entered the terrace. "I see you both have had your fill of the wine."

Abigail reached down to the table next to the recliner, took the empty flask, and turned it upside down to show that the contents were no more. "Look at this. No wine is here for us! You drank it all by yourselves."

"I am sorry, my dear," said Benrudah. "We had so many things to discuss. I didn't realize we were drinking as much as we were talking. There is more wine downstairs. Abigail, will you get some?"

"No, bother," Alexia said as she laughed, "I am only pretending with you. Abigail and I enjoyed some wine while we were inside." She turned to Yeshua, "How are you feeling, my love? You look exhausted."

"I am. It has been a long day. Too many things to think about," Yeshua said. "Let us retire for the evening. We must rest before we continue on our way."

"It is no hurry, my son," Benrudah insisted. "You are our guest for as long as you need to be."

"He is right," said Abigail. "It is so good to have another woman around to talk to and laugh with. Yeshua, you have such a beautiful and smart wife. You are blessed."

Yeshua and Alexia grinned at each other. They mutually understood that no one needed to know that they were not officially married. Not only would her father never permit such a thing to happen, but with all that had been happening, there was no time to consider a traditional betrothal. They were content with the love that bound them together. They both gave up all that they had to be with the other. There was nothing more either of them needed. After saying good evening to Benrudah and Abigail, Yeshua and Alexia took the winding staircase to their bedroom loft.

Before laying down to sleep, Yeshua held both of Alexia's hands as they kneeled on the floor. Unlike the sandy bottom of his home, the stone floor pressed hard against their knees. The soft Persian rug gave some comfort, but it only allowed them enough cushion to keep from falling over. They looked intensely into each other's eyes. The moon provided the perfect lighting for the occasion to recite the ancient pledge together:

"Intreat me never to leave you,
or to return from following after you:
for wherever you go, I will go;
and wherever you reside, I will reside:
your people will be my people,
and your God my God."[1]

---

1. Ruth 1:16–17.

NEW LIFE

The days spent in Yeriho were relaxing and reinvigorating. Days soon turned into months. Alexia and Yeshua enjoyed the comfort of Benrudah's hostel as they engaged in conversations with the various traveling merchants who passed through.

During the months in Yeriho, Yeshua made several important observations. First, his narratives were more popular than he had thought, and news about them reached well beyond the borders of the empire. Second, the character Jesus was more influential than he had predicted. Most people who stayed at the hostel had heard about Jesus—they could recount at least one of his parables and often spoke of him as if he was an actual living person.

"He is not your typical Judean man," explained one seaman who was in town delivering a load of exotic fish. "He is also not one of the ancient prophets. His wisdom was more like a Greek philosopher, and his boldness reminded me of the stories about Moses. Yet, he seems to be the gentlest and most loving human being one has ever experienced. God is truly in this man."

Yeshua made a third observation upon hearing the surprising news that the death of Jesus was not consequential to his popularity. Some travelers spoke about versions of his dramas that ended with his death. In these same dramas, Jesus returned three days later and made several appearances before the people. Some thought this was a good compromise between traditional messiah and martyrdom mythologies. Other stories did not feature either of these but focused on the impact that his message had on the actions of ordinary people. The central theme in every version focused on hope for all, Judeans and Greeks, to coexist in peace. Many Romans were also impacted by the performances and shared in their vision.

A fur trader spoke with Yeshua about how one scene revealed a different perspective about the way the emperor treated the peasants. "It was like a mirror being placed in front of me to show me who we Romans really are to the Judeans. I left the performance a changed man. I went home and set all of my slaves free."

The reports were overwhelming to Yeshua—and frightening. "It is as if I have turned the world upside down," he said late one evening to Alexia.

As the days lingered, the reality of how pervasive the Jesus story was crystalized in Yeshua's mind. The stories were giving people hope, regardless of whether there was a death scene. What started as simple street performances had become a movement enacted by various acting guilds throughout the region.

Eventually, reenactments of the Jesus story were developed by certain followers and based on the various philosophies of the artists. They named schools after their founders to help train young thespians. One school, the Lukan Academy, portrayed Jesus as a charismatic leader who performed miracles of healing. In these dramas, Jesus was literate and spoke Greek and Aramaic languages. Many of the performances were written down on papyrus and translated into Greek.

Soon it became almost impossible to tell the difference between Jesus, the character in the dramas, and Jesus the revolutionary. Roman oppression increased as the notoriety of the performances spread. The executions of some actors only incited the people to be more determined than ever to attend the performances and spread the news about a man named Jesus.

"They can kill the man, but they cannot kill the message," Yeshua once said at a gathering of local youth who heard about his fame. "Never let them divide you. You are one people. All are created in the image of the Creator. Do not let them teach you to hate yourselves or each other—love one another. When you love, hate cannot win. You are the light of the world."

The discussion with the youth took place in Yerusalem during the Passover festival. People from all over the province gathered each year to commemorate their most famous leader, Moses, who emancipated their Hebrew ancestors from Egyptian bondage. Visitors filled the streets from all parts of Asia and Africa. Students from the Lukan Academy presented the final scene of the Jesus story at the main amphitheater in the center of town.

Yeshua decided to attend the performance since it was one of the rare versions that included the death of Jesus by Roman crucifixion. He sat on the ground on a section of grass to the south of the main stage. The warm temperatures were unseasonable for that time of year, but a cool breeze made it more bearable. The intense light from the torches around the stage gave the appearance of daylight even though the night was far spent.

After the performance, many began the long walk back to their homes. Yeshua remained anonymous in the crowd of attendees as he hoped to hear people's opinions of the final scene. His attention was immediately captured by the conversation between a husband and his wife. They were from a town called Emmaus.[2]

The husband, Cleopas, expressed confusion about the death of Jesus and its meaning. "It does not make sense for the hero of the story to be killed by the Romans! The true Messiah would not have suffered such a fate," he said to his wife, Symeon. "What good is a dead prophet to the people?" .

---

2. Luke 24:13–35.

"I understand your frustration, my husband. But did you see how many people came tonight? Did you see and hear how much Jesus and his words moved them? His death seemed to empower and unite people," Symeon said as they walked toward the six-mile stretch of road from Yerusalem to Emmaus.

Yeshua was so intrigued by the questions that he followed along with them, but they did not know who he was. "Do you mind if I walk with you? I want to hear more about what you thought of tonight's performance."

Both Cleopas and Symeon thought it was odd for a stranger to want to walk with them to Emmaus, especially given the lateness of the hour. However, they both seemed relieved to have another companion for conversation and safety.

"So, tell me what you thought about the performance?" Cleopas asked Yeshua. "What do you think about the death of the main character at the hands of the enemy? Have you ever heard of anything so absurd?"

Yeshua, not wanting to take sides or reveal his identity, cautiously responded, "I see your point. But your wife's perspective and observations are undeniable. Perhaps the Jesus in the story is a different kind of leader. Maybe he is not like the ancient prophets but has a different vision for our future."

"I agree with you," Symeon said. "Times have changed. We are not living in the same conditions as our ancestors. Military leaders in the past have always proven to be corrupt and short-sighted. The one who lives by the sword will die by the sword. He is right. A military solution will never bring lasting shalom."

"You may be right," said Cleopas, "but it is the tradition. It has been taught in the Scriptures all my life. I cannot imagine another way."

"And you don't have to, my friend," Yeshua said, speaking more intensely. "What do the Scriptures say? None of us can read them. But I am convinced that the prophets had something more in mind than a simple military victory. Moses, Elijah, and Deborah had a vision of a time and a place where people lived in peace with each other. Where no one was better or of higher status than the other, and the people would share everything in common. This is in the Scriptures too. Abraham was in search of the city of peace and love, not a fortified kingdom of imperial rule."

The conversation between the three went on for several hours. As they came closer to Emmaus, Yeshua thanked them for allowing him to journey with them.

"I must continue on my way. My wife is waiting for my return," Yeshua told them.

"But sir, it is getting late into the night. It is not safe for you to be on these roads alone," said Symeon.

"My wife is right," Cleopas agreed. "Come stay with us until the morning. We are poor, but we have enough to share. It will be a blessing to us if you stay."

"Please, sir," Symeon said. "We have some fresh bread and wine. You can have a meal with us before you leave in the morning."

Although Yeshua was eager to return home to Alexia, he knew what they said about the dangers of traveling alone at night was true. Besides, it was far better to stay the night and arrive home much later than to be robbed and left for dead on the side of the road.

Early the next day, Yeshua awakened to the sun's rays bursting into the two-room tent that belonged to Cleopas and Symeon. He had never spent the night in Emmaus before. Several times, his father spoke about it as a small and quiet village where the people practiced hospitality to strangers passing through.

By the time he was fully awake, the smell of fresh bread radiated throughout the room. As Yeshua entered the tent's opening that led to the adjacent room, their pallets were already rolled up and put away. A rug was placed neatly in the center of the room with a basket of bread and a full flask of wine and fresh fish. Their generosity moved Yeshua.

"Come, my son, and sit with us." Cleopas was already seated and waving his hands for Yeshua to join them. Symeon sat down afterward with a stone bowl of fresh water to wash their hands before eating the bread. "I have thought a lot about what you said to us on the way here last night."

"Me too," said Symeon. "Our hearts were warmed by your words and vision of a new future for our people. We understand better now the message of this Jesus. It is not like the traditional vision of the previous generation. People are more diverse now and have a variety of beliefs. Our culture has changed, and we must change with it."

"My eyes have been opened. I want to thank you," said Cleopas. "I cannot thank you properly if I do not know your name."

A brief silence fell in the room. It never occurred to Cleopas or Symeon to ask the name of the stranger who walked with them. He slept all night on their floor, and was now breaking bread and drinking wine with them. He had yet to reveal who he was, nor did it occur to them to ask.

Yeshua looked across the rug at the eyes of Cleopas, who awaited an answer. Before saying anything, Yeshua reached into the basket and took the loaf of bread. He divided it into three pieces, passed one to Symeon and the other to Cleopas.

As they received the bread, he said, "I am called Yeshua ben Samuel."

"Yason?" Cleopas and Symeon said at the same time as they looked at each other and very casually responded, "Such a common name. We welcome you to our home." They both laughed.

Several years went by before Yeshua appeared in public. Petras continued to perform the role of Jesus until the emperor finally executed him. The dramas continued to be the most adored of any performed around the Mediterranean. As much as he resisted the idea of the resurrection of Jesus, it later emerged as the favorite scene among many mixed audiences. Much of this happened because of a prolific producer's work by the name of Saul of Tarsus.

As a wealthy member of the Sanhedrin, Saul financed many of Yeshua's acts and was responsible for their movement into the mainstream. Eventually, the final scene of the death of Jesus appeared at the Athens Festival of Harvest. Saul was not only the principal promoter of the resurrection philosophy, but many saw him as a shrewd financier. He seemed to understand the opportunities Hellenization offered for Judean and Roman relations.

Others simply saw Saul as a capitalistic opportunist. He frequently held meetings with some of the original actors, such as Thomas and Marco. Unbeknownst to Yeshua, Thomas had transcribed many popular lines and sold them to Saul with all reproduction rights. It was Matthew who insisted on portraying Jesus as a righteous Judean who followed ancient customs and traditions. But Saul had other motives.

"I think we have an opportunity before us to make a difference in the world," declared Saul as he exchanged the silver coins for the papyri. "The modern world needs a good story about a leader that will bring unity among all people, Judeans, Romans, and Greeks. We need a heroic model who will transcend the cultural divisions and propel us into the eschaton."

Thomas and Marco did not say anything. They handed over the papyri and took the coins. After a few moments of silence, Thomas said to Saul as he was about to leave the synagogue,

"As it is written, so shall it be."

Epilogue

"So, as the apostle Paul declared, Jesus was resurrected from the dead so that we could have eternal life. That is the most fundamental truth in the Christian message," the Sunday school teacher continued. "Can anyone here tell us what it means to you for Jesus to be alive in your life?"

The class of about fifteen adults sat in a circle around a table in the church's library. Bookcases filled with books about religious subjects like the Bible, Christian theology, and church history lined each wall of the room from end to end. Ramon spent a lot of time in class glancing over the titles of the books in the room. He often wondered if anyone actually read them. Their primary use seemed to serve as decorations, since people seldom used this space as a library.

Initially, several people objected to having a library in the church, questioning if it served any purpose. Others saw it as a waste of space when there were so many other more critical church needs. Ramon, who was not a part of the discussion or decision, often wondered if the room's multipurpose function as a Sunday school classroom, a place for special meetings, and storage space for Vacation Bible School materials reflected only the church's need to preserve its legacy. For Ramon, the decline of the congregation over the years made the discussion about the resurrection of Jesus irrelevant.

"This congregation could use a resurrection of its own," Ramon thought but was reluctant to say anything at this point in the closing moments of Sunday school.

The neighborhood changed over the years as more Hispanics and African-Americans moved in to occupy the vacant homes and church buildings left by white-flight. Many of the African-American churches were once owned by white denominations. Few of the new residents, many of whom hold low-wage jobs, attended church. Many middle-class African-Americans moved to the suburbs but continued returning on the weekends to attend church. Unlike Ramon, who still resided in the community, most only returned to the neighborhood on Sunday to attend church and visit with friends and family.

"I don't want to open that can of worms. But it makes me wonder about the point of a discussion about resurrection when we can barely keep the doors open at this church," Ramon finally spoke.

The teacher responded, "All that matters is Jesus Christ is alive today in our hearts and minds because he was crucified on the cross and raised from the dead so that we might be called the children of God. Let us all rejoice today, knowing that God will have a place for us in heaven when we die. Your sins have been forgiven for you who have believed in the resurrected Lord, Jesus Christ."

A woman in the back of the room raised her hand to speak.

"Yes, my sister," said the teacher. "Tell us all what the resurrection of Jesus means to you."

The woman slowly began to speak. First, she stood up, and everyone in the room turned to look at her. Her name was Melody Hopkins, a white female in her early fifties. Her pale skin, wrinkled jeans, and soft white t-shirt immediately differentiated her from the other class members. The blond hair resting on her shoulders had obvious signs of not being washed or conditioned for some time. She had been attending the church for a month. She once attended a white church across town, but public shame drove her away after divorcing her abusive husband. Recent mental health issues had led her to become even more isolated from friends and family. The silence in the room made it clear people were anxious about what Melody might have to say.

The teacher, sensing the impatience in the room, asked again, "Melody, do you have something you would like to say?"

Melody hesitated to speak, not knowing how people felt about her. The eyes in the room seemed to focus on her every word. Some had smiles on their faces, but Melody could see beyond their pretenses of respectability. She had learned how to read people's true intentions. Visiting mental health clinics will train a person to recognize when people were just nice to hide their true feelings. After a few moments of looking at everyone and looking down at the floor, Melody finally spoke.

"Well, I think we are all a bunch of hypocrites," she said. "You all come to church every Sunday in your fancy cars and wear your nice clothes and pass right by the people living around here. You pass them by and never say a word to them. I don't think Jesus was like that. He loved people despite their problems. He hung out in bars and visited the houses of sinners.

That's the Jesus I know. He's nothing like the Jesus you all seem to worship." Melody sat back down in her chair.

The silence continued in the room. No one offered a rebuttal or a response. They all seemed relatively unmoved by the speech. Its familiarity seemed to dampen its effect. Finally, the teacher broke the silence.

"Thank you, Melody, for those sincere words. We all have some work to do to be more like Christ," the teacher said.

People nodded, not because they agreed with Melody's assessment, but because they very much wanted the moment to pass as soon as possible.

"Now, let us all be sure to review next week's lesson. It is about Jesus and his disciples feeding the five thousand. Make sure you read the study guides and answer the questions at the end of the chapter," said the teacher as he moved the class time to its completion.

"Well, I think Melody is right," a voice sounded above the noise of people's bodies moving out of their chairs and shuffling their feet toward the exit. Everyone turned around to see who said such a thing. Sitting in the middle of the room was Ramon, defiant and demanding they all pay attention.

"We are hypocrites," he said to them. "She is right. And all of us know it. We meet each week in our little room studying our Sunday school lesson, and none of it ever penetrates our consciousness. It never challenges us to be something different. We are not like the Jesus in the Bible. We are more like the Pharisees and scribes."

"Ramon, we didn't know you felt this way. You have always seemed to enjoy our lessons. You are quiet, but never would I have known you think this way about us," said Henry, one of the oldest members of the class.

Ramon responded immediately, "It has nothing to do with what I feel about any of you. I have been thinking about this for some time. Do we know who Jesus is or only what we have been conditioned to see? Sometimes when I sit here and listen to us talk about the Bible and the things Jesus does or will do, it sounds more like a Christmas TV commercial for Santa Claus."

Henry reacted, "So what is wrong with that? Jesus is my Savior and loves me. Jesus loves everyone the same."

"Yes, you are right. But do we love Jesus and love everybody the way Jesus loves them?" asked Ramon. "When you look at Jesus for who he really was, you will see that he was more radical than most of us can accept. He was both simple and complex, conventional and countercultural, and most of all, he preferred the poor and the oppressed. That is not the Jesus we talk about in this classroom. Our Jesus fits well in our culture and is socially and culturally accommodating to our way of life. Frankly, I am tired of coming to Sunday school just to feel good and comfortable about who I am."

"Well, Ramon, maybe you should be the teacher," the teacher spoke.

"Oh, come on, Jim, I don't want your job. You are a fine teacher. I just would like something more," said Ramon.

"Ramon, I mean it. I must admit that I, too, am getting tired of teaching the same old lessons each week. I would like to hear more about your ideas. You should consider teaching us for a few weeks. I could use the rest. After a few lessons, we will talk about it and see where we go from there. What do you all think?" said the teacher to all in the class.

"I like the idea," said Carolyn.

Carolyn was a woman in her forties who was married to one of the stewards in the church. Her husband usually didn't attend Sunday school. Carolyn was self-confident and a teacher at the local high school. She was excited about the prospects of a new teacher and fresh ideas.

"Ramon, you should consider this opportunity," Carolyn said.

Ramon thought for another moment and said, "I think I will do that . . . I will do just that."

After saying this, Ramon and the others began leaving the classroom one at a time, walking past Melody as if she never existed, without giving her credit for starting the discussion. There was no more discussion about the matter. Nor was there ever another invitation for Ramon to teach the lesson.

Things stayed the same each Sunday until one day, Ramon decided to host a Bible study in his home on Saturday mornings. It was open to anyone who wanted to know more about the actual words of Jesus. At first, only a few people came to the early morning Bible studies. But after about three years, more people were attending than Ramon had room for in his house. They eventually moved the Bible studies to the local library, where the rental was free for civic and religious groups.

The gatherings also became more diverse than the Sunday school class at the church. People of different races, ethnicities, genders, sexual orientations, and economic, social, and educational backgrounds flocked to the sessions on Saturdays. Eventually, Ramon decided to divide people into small groups with common interests. He developed group leaders to help facilitate Bible discussions.

It was not very long before the small Bible study on Saturdays became a medium-sized church. Once that occurred, they started putting standards in place about who could teach and who could attend. Then, several people insisted on a single understanding of who Jesus was and is for those who believe in him. It did not take long for them to become just like the other churches. They discontinued many community outreach programs, settling for the typical inward focus of most Christian congregations.

Ramon eventually stopped attending church. On Sundays, he stayed home but continued to read and study about Jesus as he explored the many possibilities of the one called Jesus, the Judean from a place called Galilee. Often, he paused just to think a moment and ask the question, "What if?"